TIME OUT

Jamie Mason

WolfSinger Publications ~ Security Colorado

Copyright © 2021 by Jamie Mason
Published by WolfSinger Publications

All rights reserved.
No part of this book may be used or reproduced in any manner whatsoever without the written permission of the copyright owner. For permission requests, please contact WolfSinger Publications at editor@wolfsingerpubs.com

All characters and events in this book are fictitious.
Any resemblance to persons living or dead is strictly coincidental.

Cover Art copyright 2021 © Lee Ann Barlow

ISBN 978-1-944637-01-9

Printed and bound in the United States of America

The two most powerful warriors are patience and time.

— Leo Tolstoy, *War & Peace*

CONTENTS

Chapter 1: Memo from the Edge
Chapter 2: Enemies
Chapter 3: The War
Chapter 4: School of Pain
Chapter 5: Rebellion
Chapter 6: Nineteen-Sixty Something
Chapter 7: Theft
Chapter 8: Chess
Chapter 9: Every Dark Tomorrow
Chapter 10: Incense & Handcuffs
Chapter 11: Titan
Epilogue: "We are Stardust"

CHAPTER ONE
Memo from the Edge

I keep the gun at the top of my backpack so I can grab it quickly like I did last night. I was spooning a bite of shoplifted ravioli into my mouth when I heard footsteps. The silhouette of a man appeared in the mouth of the storm drain. At first, I thought he might be one of the Archon's soldiers hunting me. Turned out to be a drunk looking for a place to piss. He froze when I stood, and we had a stare-down that lasted a minute but felt like forever. Then the lights from a passing car glinted off the gun in my hand and he decided to go elsewhere.

This stretch of the interstate is pretty deserted. A small cluster of businesses where two highways intersect provides the only food and shelter for a hundred miles in any direction. It takes me an hour to walk there. I'm careful to wait until noon or sun-down so I can blend with the peak-time traffic of cops and truckers and highway homeless. I beg spare change in the lot then slip in and buy (or steal) what I need from the convenience store. So far, I haven't been caught but I have to be careful. They have surveillance cameras and I know my image, captured on video, is fed into a database that's instantly available to government, military, and law enforcement worldwide. I'm in a world of computers, where everything is interconnected.

As near as I can tell it is the year 2019 or 2020.

~ * ~

The convenience store door chimes its descending two-note welcome, and sweeps closed. Today's clerk is the Navajo kid with the thick-framed eyeglasses. He glances up long enough to verify I'm not some tumbleweed the desert blew in then resumes texting up a storm on his cellphone. I tilt my head away from the CCTV camera and make for the coolers.

Only two trucks in the lot today and the one driver I spare-changed told me to fuck off so I'm going to have to steal. And not "go for the discount" kind of stealing where you pocket one thing then pay for another, but outright theft, which means coming in with nothing and leaving with something but not paying for anything. Larceny on a high wire, without a net.

I can get the things I need pretty quickly but have to be careful because I'm the only one in the store right now. It's best to wait until the clerk is ringing someone up before boosting. I don't have to wait long. A car pulls up and a family emerges—two pot-bellied parents and a puppy-tumble of kids. A chorus of arguing voices enters. The chime goes off a half-dozen times. I make my move: two loaves of bread and a squeeze bottle of mustard go into my pack.

The kids are prowling the aisles, fiddling with merchandise, and staring at me in that dumb belligerent way little kids have. I smile back at them. The oldest boy and girl giggle and whisper to each other. I hear the word *weird*, the word *dork*.

I wait until I hear the beeping of the register keys before swiping two packets of cold cuts from the open snack cooler into my pockets. When I turn, I see…

…the mother staring at me.

Shit.

She leans forward and whispers something to the clerk, who reaches for the phone. The mother hisses for the kids and they immediately cluster around her legs.

The father meanwhile is getting agitated. An ex-military type with a beefy sunburned neck and blond brush-cut, he obviously feels he ought to be doing something. So he starts flexing and psyching himself up to come over and confront the skinny teenage shoplifter. When I step for the door, he moves to block my path.

I duck around the end of the aisle to the potato chips. As his footsteps approach, I take a deep breath and clear my mind, waiting to hear that ticking at the far edge of my consciousness. When I experience the sensation of falling, I wait for the next wave of the time-space continuum to rise and slip under it. It feels like stepping into a small, dark closet and pulling the door shut behind me.

When the father corners the end of the aisle, I am still there but tucked inside a fold in time eight seconds before, when I was somewhere else. So by the laws of physics, I can't be here now. But of course I am. Just completely invisible to him. I stay put until he gives up and leaves.

~ * ~

That evening back in the storm drain, I light a candle and make a bologna sandwich while pondering my situation.

I can run but I can't hide much longer. I thought jumping thirty-five years into the future would put me beyond the Archon's reach, but it hasn't. If anything, his power, and influence have grown since the Nineteen-Eighties. This squares with what I know about the next fifty years, when a destructive war is unleashed. The devastating violence flushes the last of my kind out of hiding and brings human civilization under the Archon's total control. But like any future, until it happens it is only a potentiality. I know it can be changed.

I've been studying the Archon's ways. He's an expert at seeing tipping points in time before anyone else and exploiting them to his advantage. I have learned how he selects critical moments in the present to deflect the future in whatever direction he chooses. He got practice by experimenting on me as I was growing up.

He's my father.

~ * ~

I'm going to fix this somehow. Writing it all down is the first step. There has to be a record. They say history is written by the winners, but it's *made* by those with the power and influence to shape it. My father has been planning to conquer this planet since arriving as a refugee eight thousand years ago. Being able to move through time as easily as a dolphin through water enabled him to master the time-streams, stage-managing history to his advantage. Humans don't stand a chance against that kind of power.

There's a lot to understand. But if I write it down, then I can at least begin to see the broad outlines. If nothing else, the story of what we are will survive so humanity can find it and perhaps figure out a way to stop him. With my backpack and this laptop computer I stole, I plan to keep moving.

Catch me if you can, dad.

CHAPTER TWO
Enemies

As soon as the traffic wakes me the next morning, I grab my backpack and scramble up the embankment to the highway. In a world where airplane reservations, bus schedules, and passenger lists are all interconnected, hitching is still the safest way to travel off-grid. I stick out my thumb, the gun a comforting weight in my backpack, and wait. Morning traffic is mostly commercial: long-haul trucks, law enforcement and state vehicles. Eventually a grey two-door sedan slows and glides to a stop a few meters past me. I note the rental company sticker. Tourists.

"Hey there young fella." The driver, in his late twenties with a blonde brush-cut, is a younger version of the retired Marine in the convenience store. "It's awful dangerous to be out hitchin' by yourself. How old are ya?"

"Fifteen," I say (which isn't true—I'm actually older but still only fifteen biologically). A plump brunette in the passenger seat cradles an infant and examines me through dark glasses.

"How far you goin'?" The man squints from me to his wife then back again. Seeking permission. She gives a subtle shrug.

"I'm going…" I almost give him a straight answer, but finally say: "East."

"Us too. Hop in." I slip in beside a pile of luggage. He pulls out carefully into traffic. "I'm Richard Parker. That's Cindy and my son's name is Zach. What's yours?"

"Chris." I don't offer a last name.

"Well, Chris. Must say. You're kinda young to be out here all by yourself. You run away from home?"

"No," I say. Which is true. The place I ran away from is definitely not home.

"So where're your folks?" He's watching me in the rear-view. The protective father, and I am a stranger in close quarters with his family and he expects answers. Being the focus of his suspicion, I wonder what it must be like to be on the other side of that protective wall. Zach is lucky.

"Well I'm headed homeward," I say, knowing it's an answer that will calm him a bit. And it's not entirely untrue.

Zach bursts into a bout of fussing.

Richard grins. "It's tough being sick when you're little."

"I know," I say. "I was a sickly kid."

What I don't say is that my father deliberately made me that way.

~ * ~

Nobody was sick as often as me. Except Davey. I became friends with him because we spent so much time parked next to each other in the waiting room at the Doctor's office.

"Goo—kemia," he said when I asked, at age five, what he had.

Human beings are so fragile. So prone to illness and death. Father says it's because they're weak but he's wrong. Their fragility—and their perseverance in the face of it—is part of what makes them strong.

Davey's mother sat with that look of terrible resignation on her face day after day in the waiting room. Until she stopped coming.

I didn't know what death was.

None of us do.

I should have known something was up by the mists and vapors that hung in the doctor's office, by the way the walls shimmered after he shut the door. Other doctors' offices didn't behave that way. This was because Doc was one of us.

"Miriam," he would say to Mother, "you shouldn't be doing this to him."

"I know," Mother would say, "but it's what his father wants."

And it was. He wanted me to be sick to observe the effect it would have on me if I didn't Tip. And the effect was a constant low-level fever occasionally exploding into nausea and delirium and pains that wracked my body for days on end.

~ * ~

Richard Parker carefully navigates the cramped parking lot. A spot opens when a pick-up truck backs out near where the motel units meet the entertainment complex and Richard is quick to claim it. He shuts off the ignition with a grateful sigh. We are at one of those truck-stop/casino combinations so common in this state and it is extraordinarily busy.

"We're gonna rest here for the night, Chris." He examines me across his seat back for a long moment. "You are welcome to have dinner with us as our guest. The good Lord says we're to feed the hungry and welcome the stranger amongst us and I figure you qualify."

"Thanks, but..." The sleek fixtures and tinted glass windows of the place suggest electronic video surveillance galore. "There's still plenty of daylight left, thanks. Think I'll travel on."

"Don't let the light fool ya'. Be nightfall in another two, three hours. Desert's cold after dark."

"I know it. I'll be okay."

"Need a few dollars?" He digs in his hip pocket. "Listen, let me—"

"No." I hold up my hand and walk away fast. He calls out something that might be "good luck," but I pretend not to hear and slip around back to the swimming pool. Satisfied there are no cameras, I take a seat on one of the lounge chairs.

It would feel so nice to pull off my shoes and socks and dip my feet into the water. I have a bathing suit and could probably get away with a swim before the hotel staff noticed but I better not risk it. So far, I've managed to remain one step ahead of everyone hunting me by keeping on the move. There is an open stretch of desert between here and the interstate. From the position of the sun it's possible to see the far lane runs east. That's where I start the next leg of my journey.

The door to the motel opens and a group of kids emerge in a tangle of shouting, shoving high spirits. Three girls and two guys, roughly nine, ten years old. They drop their towels and cannonball into the water as two men slip out behind them, talking quietly and lighting cigarettes. The dads, sent to supervise as the moms did whatever. One takes a good long look at me and nudges his friend. Now they're both staring at me, talking quietly. Time to go. I shoulder my backpack and step into the desert.

The sound of the kids joshing and fighting in the pool recedes behind me. Reminds me of when I was their age. My parents' idea of friends, like their ideas about so many other things, was very different from mine. They never told me Uncle Leo, with his thundering voice and ham-sized biceps and tattoos, and Em, with her mousy hair and glasses, were aliens like us. I was clueless about all of this. But I figured it out. What hurt was their daughters knew and I didn't.

I'll never forget my first look at Tara and Dis. Two little blonde twins aged eight years to my six. Something about them as they stood watching me, holding hands. In outward form like little human girls. But their eyes on me were those of cats watching a bug scuttle past.

"Hello, Chris," said Tara, the older by seventeen minutes. She introduced herself and her sister, spelling the latter's name for me. "D—I—S, her name is Dis. Do you know your alphabet, Chris?"

I admitted I knew a little bit.

"Then why don't you go over to the blackboard and show us?" Tara indicated the toy-sized chalkboard propped on a tripod in a corner of their room. "But be careful you don't fall."

"Why would I fall?"

"Because you're going to be startled by the sound of my father laughing and trip over my soccer ball."

I blinked. Half-turned toward her. Heard Uncle Leo laugh (a great, booming sound like artillery fire) and stumbled. A blur of motion ending when my chin smacked the chalk tray.

More laughter. I shook my head and sat up.

The girls were still there, but in a different place. I hadn't heard them move. They were standing, in fact, in a doorway I hadn't heard open. Still holding hands. Giggling, now. How much time had passed? Fifteen seconds? Ten? And how had they known I would...?

"You're an idiot, Chris," Tara said giggling.

"An idiot," Dis chimed in.

How had they *known*?

The bedroom they shared became my schoolhouse in the world's cruel ways.

"Read this," Tara would say, and scrawl A-P-P-L-E on the board. She always got to play the teacher. Once I read it aloud, she asked, "What is it?"

"It's a fruit. Something you eat."

"Good. And this?" She scrawled: D-O-G.

"A warm, furry animal. Something you feed and play with."

She smirked. "Sure, I suppose. Okay. Now how about this?"

C-H-R-O-N-O-X.

My six-year-old tongue stumbled.

"What is that? I've never heard of it." I was eager to learn, the way a starving man is eager to eat.

"Of course you haven't heard of it." Tara beamed with the power of information known but withheld. "You don't know because you're stupid."

Laughter from the living room outside. Our parents were drinking again.

I stamped my foot. "I am not stupid! Am not!"

Tara folded her arms. "Oh, yeah? Well, Dis isn't as smart as me and even *she's* brighter than you. Dis? What color shirt will the driver of the taxicab be wearing?"

"What taxicab?" I demanded.

"The one that's going to pull up at that house across the street in three minutes," Tara replied, as if telling me the most obvious thing in the world.

Dis grinned and disappeared into the closet. Two seconds later, she was back.

"A white and gold shirt sewn with beads!" she cried. "And he's gonna' be a black man."

We huddled around the window.

"You're so stupid, Chris," Tara complained. "I don't know if we should let you be friends with us."

I fidgeted. How could Dis claim to know what color shirt the taxicab driver would be wearing? For that matter, how could Tara claim to know a taxicab was even going to arrive in the first place? They were playing make-believe, I thought, confident I had them at last.

"I don't wanna' be your friend, anyway," I snapped.

Tara and Dis giggled. "Oh, but you will," Tara assured me. "When we're all older, like our mom and dad and Auntie Miriam and Uncle Andrew. We'll *have* to be friends. Because no one else will understand."

"Understand what?"

"The Chronox."

"That's a made-up word! A made-up, make-believe word you invented just to make *fun* of me! Because you're *mean*."

But it wasn't made up. Any more than the taxicab that suddenly pulled into the driveway across the street. Or the Rastafarian behind the wheel, who paused to scratch an itch under the armpit of his beaded white shirt.

"Stupid," whispered Tara. "Stupid, stupid, stupid Chris."

~ * ~

I stop a few yards from the highway, fists and jaw clenched, shaking with rage.

Stupid, stupid, stupid Chris…

It was the beginning of a life-long torture, one that would extend into adolescence and continue until just a few days ago when I escaped the Facility.

Enough!

I march to the highway and stick out my thumb. The sun has begun to set, throwing long shadows across the desert. I don't have to wait long. A white two-door sports coupe slows and pulls up beside me. The driver, a blonde-haired woman in her early twenties, rolls down the passenger window.

"Get in, Chris," says Tara, pointing a gun at me.

CHAPTER THREE
The War

"I've got him."

Tara speaks tersely into her cellphone before pulling back into traffic. A Highway Patrol cruiser overtakes us and assumes position two car lengths ahead, activating its flashers. A blast of red light in the rear-view tells me a second cruiser has done the same behind us. Tara chuckles.

"Stupid, stupid, stupid Chris."

"How did you find me?"

"You're not very smart. It wasn't hard."

"No really. He told you, didn't he?"

"We didn't have to disturb him." Tara's right eye twitches just enough to tell me she's lying. We follow the lead cruiser as it turns down a dirt road into the desert.

"You weren't smart enough to figure it out on your own."

"Shut up you little brat." Tara squints into the brown plume the cruiser raises.

"Stupid, stupid, stupid Tara…"

"Grow up!"

"I would if you'd let me!"

A dark shape appears ahead. The Highway Patrol cruiser has pulled into the parking lot of what resembles an abandoned gas station. Tara brakes to a stop.

"Get outta the car, Chris. Don't run or I'll put a bullet in you."

"You'd like that, wouldn't you?"

The second cruiser pulls up. Highway Patrol officers are standing at the edge of the parking lot. I get out of the car and shoulder my backpack.

"This way!"

We march toward a wide concrete pad. Some sort of building, possibly a large structure like a hotel, once stood here. A low thrum rises behind the mountain as we step onto the vast rectangle.

"I'll take that." Tara yanks my backpack from me. She peels down the zipper and begins sorting through clothes. "What have we here?" She pulls the revolver free and brandishes it. "Good thing I found this. You might have tried to use it and hurt yourself."

"Fuck you."

The thrum materializes overhead, expanding from a bug-like speck into an unmarked black military helicopter that lowers itself with a deafening roar and blast of propwash. A hatch on the side springs open the moment it touches down. Tara shoves me into motion.

No point in resisting. I am hauled up through the hatch and strapped into a bucket seat. A minute later, the chopper plunges skyward.

~ * ~

I was instructed to write a report about my family history for fourth grade social studies. My father wasn't speaking to me that day, so I consulted Mother instead.

"Where do we come from?"

Mother was ironing shirts on a blanket folded across the dryer. "Why do you want to know?"

"I have to write a report for school."

She paused, the iron hissing to a stop halfway down a shirt-sleeve. "We're—ah—from out of town."

I picked up my pencil. "Where?"

The iron hisses down the sleeve. "Far away."

"And how did we end up here?"

"We're refugees. We came because of the war."

"Oh?" I grew excited. There was a *war* in my past! "What war? Was it a big one?"

"Oh, yes. It was very big. *Huge.*" Her gaze grew distant. "I remember...waking up one morning. And the entire sky was burning. At first, I thought it was sunrise, but mother said no, it was gas igniting in the atmosphere."

"Your mom? That would be...grandma?"

"Yes, I suppose."

"I've never met her. Why not?"

"She died before the refugee ship left."

"Oh. What was the name of the war?"

Mother said nothing.

I grew impatient. "They'll *ask*, you know..."

"Just tell them it's a word they couldn't pronounce."

"Okay." I wrote this down. "Did a lot of people die?"

"Oh, yes. My. Lots and lots. Whole worlds…"

"Worlds? You mean like planets?"

"Ah—I meant peoples' entire *worlds* were destroyed. That's what I meant."

"What was the war about?"

"Oh, well…the same thing wars are always about."

"Freedom?"

"No. Control of resources."

"What resources? Like, space?"

Mother laughed. "No, there was plenty of space. *Time* was the thing in short supply."

"I don't get it."

She flicked her eyes right, then left. "Some things," she said quietly, "exist in space, while others exist in time. Some exist in both; the way human beings do. But most tend to exist in either one or the other. So if you exist in *time*, it doesn't matter if you have all the *space* you need. If you're running out of time, you're in trouble."

"And that's what happened to us?"

"That's what happened to your father and I. What's happening to *you* is very different."

"What's a Chronox?"

"Don't *ever* let your father hear you say that word!"

~ * ~

Tara produces her cellphone and busies herself with e-mail while a trio of special operations guys in tinted helmets and black jumpsuits watch me. Dusk. The chopper climbs to its cruising altitude and flies for forty-five minutes before descending over the fence-line of a high-security military reservation. Night falls and the runway lights of the Air Force base wink to life. We touchdown and a blast of light from approaching vehicles fills the hatch window.

Tara breaks away from the group and boards an electric passenger cart emblazoned with the Nellis Airbase/Area 51 logo driven by a female airman. "Take him to the Archon," she says. The airman drives off. I am escorted into the Humvee and taken to the windowless concrete building which houses the Facility.

Like the guards onboard the helicopter, my escort wears a

black jumpsuit and carries a submachine gun. He says nothing as we make our way through the low-ceilinged corridors of Sector T-23 past mostly engineers in white coats or uniformed Air Force personnel. Nobody even glances at me.

I feel the familiar crushing implosion in my chest that precedes any conversation with Father. Knowing, before even opening my mouth, I will be defeated and destroyed. What purpose does any discussion between us serve except as an opportunity for him to reduce me to ruins?

The walls transition from concrete to glass, then from glass to mahogany. We pass through an empty reception area emblazoned with the TimeSygn corporate logo. A suite of offices. Shaded light and voices from within: Father's and Uncle Leo's. The guard and I stand against the wall. Soon a green light flashes on a panel above the door.

"Go in."

The first thing I notice crossing the threshold is the increased height of the ceiling. It is a long walk across the vast sanctum of Father's office to where he sits reading a document in the light of a shaded banker's lamp. He speaks without looking up:

"Now do you see what happens when you disobey me?"

I say nothing.

"Answer me!"

"You locked me up here. I ran. Am I supposed to apologize for that?"

"Getting bold now, aren't you? Don't get too cocky, Chris. We can still hurt you." He flashes a smile. "*I* can still hurt you."

"Everyone needs a hobby."

"You have no idea what you're jeopardizing here. All of the work your Uncle Leo and I have put into developing the technology. The importance of it to the government—to *us*—is just.... Well, probably beyond your capability to understand. You think I'm a bad man?"

"I think you're a vicious bastard."

"Oh you do, do you? You should have met my stepfather. Know what he did to me? When I was eleven, I sassed him. He retaliated by pushing me back five years to the age of six and making me relive those same years all over again. It was terrible, repeating ages six to eleven with my memories intact, unable to change a thing.

Really tough!"

I say nothing.

"I suggest you don't try running away again, Chris. We've doubled the guard. And repaired the grating on that air-duct you crawled out through. I've also consulted with Major Gordon. He agrees additional activity will do you some good. So I've arranged for you to engage in some recreational sports with Airman Ryerson."

"Airman *Ryerson*? She's like…Hitler!"

"Hitler wasn't so bad. I met him. Spent a pleasant afternoon at the Kehlsteinhaus with him and Goëring. Helped get us where we are now."

Hitler wasn't so bad? "When your father did that thing to you. Did you learn anything?"

"Yes. I learned to hide things better."

I smile because I have a few secrets of my own these days.

A door opens and Airman Ryerson appears, blonde and crisp and grey-eyed in her sharp-creased Air Force blues. She steps up and claps a hand on my shoulder. And not in a friendly way.

"Take him back to Major Gordon, please."

"Yessir."

"I want him to begin his training immediately."

"Yessir."

"And make sure you're thorough."

"Sir!"

I am hauled from the office and conducted back upstairs to the van. Airman Ryerson smirks at me from the jump-seat as we cross the darkened airbase.

"Well, well. The little prince."

"Does that make you my wicked stepmother?"

"You have no idea, Chris. But you'll learn. Notice we're alone. No armed guards."

"Obviously, you're capable of handling me on your own."

"I am. You have no idea."

But I'll learn. A fast transfer in the company of armed guards through the lobby of an office complex, then an elevator down a dozen floors. Ryerson remains at my side during the march down the familiar concrete hallway to my dorm. Fred, the guard who is usually on duty at this hour, greets me with a nod before keying in the code to unlock my quarters.

"Wait here." Is it my imagination or is Ryerson breathing heavily? "And Chris? I suggest you prepare yourself mentally."

"For what?"

"Pain. Lots of it."

The door slides shut. Peace and quiet floods me, offset by disappointment. I have nice quarters at the Facility, but I don't want to be here. I begin pacing. Everything is as I left it, the little kitchenette neat and scrubbed, the bathroom glowing dimly with its nightlight, the flat-screen in the living room set to a screensaver of an autumn forest, the guitar by the bed-side table, the pile of dog-eared paperback books stacked nearby: Sun-Tzu, Von Clausewitz, Rommel's *On Attack* and Julius Caesar's memoir of Gaul.

The door chime sounds—a cosmetic courtesy, as Facility personnel can just walk in any time they please. But some psychologist suggested it might be a good way to off-set the corrosive stress of being imprisoned. The door slides open onto Major Gordon's sad smile.

"Tara asked I give you this." He hands over the backpack. "And Airman Ryerson sends this." He extends a white bundle. A slow uneasiness creeps over me. The bundle is a folded gi, a traditional martial arts uniform.

"I didn't know you were interested in karate."

"I'm not."

"Chris," Major Gordon takes a seat on the edge of the desk. "I'm glad you're okay. After we learned you'd escaped, I was plenty worried. You could have been shot."

I say nothing; merely open the backpack and sort through the clothes. The gun, of course, is gone but my fingers find the straight edge of the laptop. I pry it loose and boot it up.

"Chris, I think it's important you give up this idea of trying to escape and focus on your schoolwork. I only have another three months to prep you for your GED and it's not an easy exam. Your father is pretty insistent you be ready to start making a contribution around here, and the regs require a minimum of a high-school or GED equivalent."

I nod, absorbed in the web of software crawling to life on my laptop window. There is a message in bold red letters on my desktop:

FOUND YOUR DIARY AND DELETED IT.

STUPID, STUPID, STUPID CHRIS.
T.

Sure enough the sham text document I had in the My Documents folder is gone. But I find this memoir still intact tucked into the machine language root directory. Tara, refusing to turn to human Facility personnel for help must have searched the unit herself. I give thanks for her arrogance and switch off the laptop with a grin.

"...have to get through the next three units of algebra by Friday and this physical education program will cut into our course time. Chris, I feel for you. You're in a very difficult position. You're completely isolated—from base personnel, from your own kind, your own family, even. I know there's a natural inclination under such circumstances to rebel. Hell, I understand! I totally understand. But you're up against more than the average teen. I'd be doing the wrong thing if I didn't urge you to reconsider. Just put your head down and do as you're told. Get through this and—"

"Major Gordon, I have to change into my karate suit."

He bites his lip and stares at the floor. "Okay. We'll talk more tomorrow." He produces a remote control from his pocket and thumbs the button that opens my dormitory door. Once he is gone, I begin undressing.

I've never been a big one for sports. And martial arts are a category all their own, one completely beyond my realm of experience. But I am familiar enough with its basic concepts to believe pain and fatigue are used to mold the body into a fighting machine. Airman Ryerson, who has never liked me, will no doubt push this practice to its extreme. I master my fear as I tug the draw-string tight on the cotton pants, drape the jacket around my shoulders and tie the belt as best I can.

Fred has been replaced by a sharp-faced young guard with a brush-cut whom I've named the Fox. The Fox is all business—strictly by the book. No smile, no banter with the Subject as he escorts me down the hall. We stop at a steel door which the Fox opens with a swipe card to reveal a stairwell. We descend and emerge into a corridor in a sector of the Facility unfamiliar to me.

The Fox leads me past a glass-walled room inside which an army of white-coated technicians labor over something resembling a moving walkway like the ones in airports. The lab is the last thing I see before we halt before a steel door, which the Fox pushes open to reveal a bare concrete storeroom.

Airman Ryerson is clad in a white gi that is identical to mine except for the black belt around her middle. She is dancing. Or perhaps not so much dancing as fighting an invisible opponent. Her moves—kicks, strikes and blocks—resemble choreography but are executed with such force and precision the room hums with menace. Airman Ryerson is an attractive woman, with her blonde hair and sharp cheekbones below sea-green eyes. But, watching her do these karate moves is not beautiful. Instead, it inspires a dread inside me like watching a cobra or tiger being set lose at close range. As I watch she twists her hips, launches into a final spinning back kick, then lands, bare feet slapping the cement. She executes a loud shout. The room swallows the echo of her cry and she pauses for a moment and collects her breathing before turning to face me.

"Welcome, student." She smiles, nods to the Fox, who pulls the door shut, leaving me alone in the room with this cobra, this tiger.

"You're going to teach me?"

"No. I'm going to *hurt* you." She raises her fists and begins to stalk me. "Hurt you like you've never been hurt before, little prince. This is old-school karate, the way they do it back in Okinawa. No gloves, no pads, no mouthguards. That stuff is for sissies. In here it's survival of the fittest. You'll either learn to defend yourself. Or get crippled."

Hurt you like you've never been hurt before. Her first punch slips through my upraised arms to slam my cheekbone and I stagger, exhaling a gust of anguished laughter. Dangerous as she is, Ryerson has no hope of hurting me as deeply as my own kind. She has no idea.

No idea at all.

CHAPTER FOUR
School of Pain

I was nine.

Peter lived across the street. We were inseparable at the beginning of that summer. School out, the furnace of June not yet upon us, our world became a free and easy glide from swimming pools to neighborhood bike rides to the good smells of burgers cooking on grills at twilight. At night we stared up at the stars from the lawn of somebody's backyard and wondered about dreams, aliens, the future.

Peter was special to me. He didn't go to my school, and that was just fine with me. Where I had been isolated there, in his company I felt accepted—even celebrated. Peter laughed at my jokes, enjoyed the same TV shows and comic books as me. When he found two Silver Surfer decals in a package of chewing gum, he gave one to me and we used them in exactly the same position on the front wheel-guard of our bikes.

There were other kids in the neighborhood we roamed with. We let Matt and David play with us (so long as they followed our rules) but Peter and I were protective of what we had. Our friendship was special. So when Peter's dad announced he was taking us all up to his cabin for the weekend, it was important to us that Matt and David understand: the coveted rumble seat in Pete's family's station wagon was reserved for *us*.

"Make sure you have your mom call me," Peter's mother said, handing me a slip of paper with her number on it. "We're leaving right after dinner."

"Okay!"

I ran home, the soles of my running shoes slapping cement in the wet, lawn-scented afternoon. I burst into our house.

"Mom! Guess what? Peter's *dad* is taking us up to his *cabin*!"

Mother, preoccupied, took the slip of paper I handed her and placed it on a corner of the washing machine.

"You gonna' call her?"

"Yes, yes," she sighed. And went back to ironing shirts.

Pushing Mother when she spoke in that weary voice was a

non-starter. Best to let her sit at the kitchen table and smoke some cigarettes before trying again. So I made my way to the fridge. Pulled it open. Took a swig of milk directly from the carton.

Father was at the counter, the pieces of some mechanical device (a radio? a soldering gun?) strewn before him. He said:

"Don't bother your mother."

I bit back my initial reply ("I wasn't!") in favor of a more contrite, "I won't."

His dark eyes shot toward me. "What was it you wanted?"

"Peter's dad is taking us up to his *cabin*! Me and Peter and Matt and David! It's going to be *great*!"

Dad frowned at me in that way he had of pinning the world in place while he examined it, tilting it this way and that. Probing for weaknesses. It was a smile I didn't yet understand but had begun to fear.

He said, "Chris, this is something you really want. Isn't it." It wasn't a question.

"Yes!"

"Right then." He looked at the clock. So I did, too.

The big hand was on the five and the little hand was on the two.

Father pursed his lips. "Go into the workshop and get me the Philips head."

"What's that?"

"The screwdriver with the blue handle. It's on the workbench beside the vise. Go now."

Still flush with excitement, I floated across the kitchen, visions of hikes and fishing trips filling my head, through the pantry alcove and across the wooden threshold smelling of oiled metal into the dim workshop. The afternoon sun swam in around the edges of paint cans clustered on the windowsill. I stepped to the workbench, scanning for the Philips head. I sensed Father move into the doorway behind me.

The walls shimmered and undulated the way I remembered them doing in the doctor's office when I was very young. I reached for the workbench, light-headed, afraid I was going to pass out and held myself up by its edge. I blinked, searching for something I could use to anchor myself in this reality. And fastened on the paint cans in the windowsill.

A wave of Theremin sound dopplered in my ears. The bars of sunlight spearing through the cans narrowed and mellowed from bright gold to orange. By the time I caught my breath and stood upright, the screwdriver clutched in my fist, they had weakened to become pale beams sprinkled with shimmers of dust. I hurried back through to the kitchen.

Mom and Dad were gone.

The countertop was bare, no trace of the strewn components he had been tinkering with.

The big hand of the clock was on the two, the little hand on the five.

I hurled myself at the kitchen window.

Across the street, Peter's mom was hauling a suitcase toward the open hatch-back of their family station wagon. Matt and David stood to one side, back-packs at their feet, while Peter scanned the front of our house, searching for me.

"Dad! Mom!" I finally found the two of them curled up under the blankets, empty wine glasses on the table beside them.

"They're leaving!"

"Who's leaving? Honestly, Chris, I don't understand your need to shout…"

"It's his friends," Father said boredly. "That family camping trip or whatever. Chris, you're *sure* you really want to go?"

"Yes!"

"Did you call Peter's parents?"

"No." Mother pulled herself upright, hand rising to push back her hair. "Where did I put that number?"

"On the washing machine! I'll get it!"

I ran, the fading light my enemy. I seized the slip of paper from where it lay among a clutch of lint on the floor by the dryer and sprinted back. Mother was belting on a housecoat and stuffing her feet into slippers.

"Hurry," I muttered. "Hurry."

"Chris, don't tell me to hurry. You have the paper? Okay. Now…where are my glasses?"

Father lay in bed, smiling that probing-for-weakness smile, the one I did not yet understand but had begun to fear.

Outside, Peter's father was pulling the hatch-back shut.

Come on, come on! my brain screamed as I heard Mother clop down the hall toward the phone. I bolted into my room, dumping end-of-the-year supplies from my schoolbag, and grabbing a few items of clothing. I panted; certain I would make it if I just *willed* myself across the street in time.

I stepped into the hallway.

Again: the shimmering undulation, the blurred *wah* of the Theremin sound thrumming in my ears. Light sickened from dusk grey to lamp-lit pools of ebony. Shadows clustered.

"Peter!"

I made it to the entry hall, disregarding everything in my haste that would matter later: mother's confusion, Father's smile razoring at me through the dark, the clock in the hall that said quarter to six. All I knew was the opening door, the smacking of my feet, the smell of road and the taillights of a station wagon disappearing into the night.

~ * ~

Once each week, I am escorted under guard to the Facility clinic to undergo a thorough medical examination. Fred usually brings me. But the morning after my beating from Airman Ryerson, a different guard appears at my door. I drag my sore and battered body from the couch and limp down the corridor to the elevator. My ribs ache slightly when I inhale, and my left knee clenches each time it accepts weight. I note, in the stainless-steel elevator door, the bruise under my right eye has yellowed to the moldy brown of a rotting banana.

The base medical center serves a variety of functions, from decontamination to viral and biological weapons testing to routine—as well as not-so-routine—medical exams. Down one side of the corridor is a set of examination rooms like you'd see in a regular doctor's office. My doctor's office isn't one of them. Instead, my guard brings me to a pressurized steel door across the hallway and pauses as a nurse in a face mask twists a small copper steering wheel. The rubber seal breaks and the door parts with a sigh of pressurized air.

I am always brought to the same examining room. Like a regular doctor's office, it contains an examination table, a counter with a sink and a storage area for instruments. But that's where the resemblance to ordinary human medicine ends. One whole side of the room is tinted glass behind which lurks a battery of cameras and computers. A containment chamber squats by the rear wall. Resembling a large propane tank, it is designed to prevent unwilling Chronox patients from escaping into the Discontinuity.

A doctor enters with several trainees. All wear hazmat suits.

"This one's a little different." The doctor gestures vaguely in my direction. "He served as the primary test subject for the machine we're developing down on Level Two."

"Wait a minute, doctor. Are you saying the Air Force was able to obtain a *Chronox* test subject?" Astonishment bubbles in the trainee's voice.

"Ah—no." The doctor pauses to attach a blood pressure cuff to my arm before continuing. "The technology was actually prototyped by the Chronox themselves. The one they call the Archon? This is his son."

"Now I'm confused too." The second trainee to speak is female. "The Chronox move through time naturally. How could using one help develop a Discontinuity mechanism for human use?"

"That's where this one is special." The doctor pumps the bulb that tightens the cuff around my arm then takes my pulse as he explains. "The Chronox who reproduced after arriving on Earth had to teach their children how to access the Discontinuity. See, in their natural state, the Chronox exist in time *only*, not in space *and* time the way humans do. When they fled to Earth and assumed human form, they retained the ability to move through time. But their offspring had to be taught to access this same capability. Like a species that evolves legs and walks out of the ocean, after they spend enough time on dry land, their children will retain the ability to breathe underwater but won't know how. They have to be taught—reminded by their birth parents. That's how it is with the Chronox and time travel."

The assembled trainees listen, rapt.

"This boy, Chris, was never taught how to enter the Discontinuity." The doctor taps my knees with a small rubber hammer, each jumps obediently. "This was an intentional choice on the part of his family."

"Why?" The first trainee produces a notebook and pen and begins writing.

"Because by preventing Chris from developing this ability—

from accessing that part of his genetic heritage, the Archon ensured his son remained a mostly-human Chronox. A bridge, if you will, between our two species. One who could be experimented upon in developing the technology that eventually became the Discontinuity mechanism down on Level Two."

A murmur of surprise passes among the group.

"Obviously, the Chronox operate under a very different set of ethics from our own."

I somehow manage not to scream.

~ * ~

After the disappointment of that summer trip with Peter. After my father's manipulation of time to prevent me from joining my friends. After their return from a journey in which they had bonded, and I was left outside—my world changed.

And, I learned something—time makes noise.

Time filled with activity and purpose hums along like a well-tuned engine. Throw a wrench in the works and it clanks forward, slipping gears now and then. Sit in a hospital waiting room or a theater before the curtain goes up and it bubbles like the regulator on an aquarium. Endure a succession of days alone after months of stimulating companionship, and time makes a sound like the sun crossing a cement parking lot.

For a while, I felt anger at being excluded from Peter's world. A blinding red frustration when I watched him, and his two new best friends ride away up the block on their bikes. Once I overcame my anger at their forbidding me to join them, the rage settled into a dull acceptance. Then emptiness. Then time slowed from a bubbling regulator to a crawling sunbeam. To the basso drone of a planet orbiting a dead star.

My world stopped in its tracks and re-directed.

The basso drone echoed in the backseat of our car later that summer as it crawled the dirt road toward Uncle Leo's and Aunt Em's cottage. I hadn't seen Tara and Dis for a while, and part of me was actually looking forward to it. I was lonely enough to have forgotten how they were. (And, when I remembered, optimistic enough to hope they had changed.)

"Hello, Chris," they said, standing hand in hand as I stepped from the car.

I smiled at them. "It's nice to see you again," I said. And meant it.

Tara asked: "Are you still as stupid as you used to be?"

My smile faltered.

"What is going to come driving down that road in fifty-eight seconds?" I scrambled frantically for an answer.

"Come on, come on!" she snapped. "Even *Dis* can figure that one out! Dis?"

On cue, Tara's little sister slipped behind a tree, emerging a few seconds later.

"*I* know," Dis giggled. "But I want to see if *Chris* does, before I tell!"

"I know," I said, bluffing.

Tara's eyes narrowed. She wasn't accustomed to disobedience. This was a variation on her tried and true game she hadn't seen before.

"Prove it!"

"Why should I?" I smiled, swaggering a little as I stepped toward her. "What's in it for me, Tara?"

But where I had grown adept at playing the games of human children, Tara had learned other kinds. She closed her eyes and gritted her teeth.

The basso drone echoed in the backseat of our car later that summer as it crawled the dirt road toward Uncle Leo and Aunt Em's cottage. I hadn't seen Tara and Dis...

Wait a minute!

...for a while, and part of me was actually looking forward to it. I was lonely enough...

I've been here before!

...to have forgotten how they were. (Or, if I remembered, optimistic enough to hope they had changed.)

This has already happened once before!

"Hello, Chris," Tara said, standing hand in hand with her sister as I stepped from the car. "Have you learned your lesson now?"

I bit my lip, struggling to maintain her gaze.

"I can do that to you any time I want. And I can do *other* things, too!"

I said nothing. Glanced over at my parents, chatting amiably with Aunt Em and Uncle Leo.

"Now *tell* me." Tara smiled. "*What* you think is coming down that road in fifty-eight seconds."

"I...I don't know."

"Tha-a-t's right. Because you're...? Say it."

I said nothing.

Her eyes widened as she stared me down, preparing to grit her teeth and hurl me back into the past.

So I said, very quietly, "I'm stupid."

~ * ~

Faced with a power I could neither understand nor oppose, I fell obediently into line behind Tara. That sole demonstration of her strength was enough. I never challenged her again. I learned to fake illness instead. Uncle Leo's property consisted of a number of small buildings to which I could retreat. Tara would ask, "What's going to happen next?" Dis would say she knew, and I would say I didn't. Then Tara would call me stupid, and I would smile.

I feel sick, I would say. And vanish, spending enough time huddled on a couch or sleeping mattress in an out-building to allay Tara's suspicions before going for a walk in the woods.

I was beginning to put it together.

The undulating walls in the doctor's office. Tara's and Dis' "game". The events of that day Peter's family left for the cottage. There was some strange power at work in my life. But what? My mind drifted back to mother's story of our family's refugee flight, and her remarks about creatures living in time as opposed to space. Had she meant *us*? Was it possible we were from another world?

Chronox...

The woods led down to a lake. There was a stone beach. Gray boulders wept at the edge of the tideline. Musk filled the pine-shrouded wilderness; the air was alive with scent.

Then, sound. A guitar.

A girl sat at the end of a small wooden pier. Older than me—probably sixteen or seventeen. Jeans. Sleeveless black t-shirt. Bare feet. Strumming a guitar. She turned when my sneakers scuffed the gravel behind her. A narrow face topped by short strands of black hair. Bright eyes. A friendly grin.

"Hey there, little man."

"Hi. Um, that's nice music you're playing."

"Thanks. Do you wanna' come and sit with me?"

I nodded. She moved over to make room. I noticed a paperback book. *Dune*.

"Is this science fiction?" I asked, picking it up and examining the cover. Sand. Guys in space suits.

"Yeah." She strummed a chord. "You like that kind of stuff?"

"I do." I hefted the paperback. Discouraged by its weight, I put it back. "It's a big book."

"It's a complicated story."

I examined her get-up. "Are you a hippie?"

She had to stop strumming long enough to get hold of herself again.

"Wow, that's funny. Am I a hippie? Nah. That's, like, twenty years ago or more. I think. What year is it, anyway?"

"I have no idea."

"Now *you* sound like a hippie." She plucked a cigarette from behind her ear and a book of matches from her pocket. "I'm gonna' smoke now. Okay?"

"Okay."

She lit up and dragged. After a while, she handed the cigarette to me. I took a puff but didn't inhale.

"What's your name?"

"Lu. It's funny you think I'm a hippie. What's your name?"

"Chris. Why's it funny?"

"Just is." She played a few notes, staring out at the lake. "I s'pose I believe some of the same things hippies do; now that you mention it. And I smoke weed and play guitar. But that don't mean nothing. Used to be if you played guitar, you were special. Now all it means is you're a Democrat. And everybody smokes weed, anymore."

"Hippies believe in things?"

"Well, I guess…I dunno'." She sucked a lungful of its aromatic smoke. "Maybe it's like…hippies *used* to believe in things. Actually, this is something I'm very interested in…. How, once upon a time, like, hippies all believed in things. But now they're all real estate investors and dentists and politicians and all they give a shit about is money, anymore. Same as everybody else. Guess that's how time works. You start out as one thing and become another. And the things you believe in change, too. Or they *can*. That's why I think time is the most powerful force in the universe. And that we'll never conquer it."

I said nothing.

"Don't get me wrong, though. I think the ideals of the hippies were *good* things. If you sort through the bullshit, what it boiled down to was being open-minded."

I picked up the book and examined it with new interest.

"You can borrow that, if you want." Lu stood, flicked her cigarette into the lake and swung the neck of her guitar over one shoulder. "And you can come visit again."

"When?"

"Anytime you like. My mom and I live in that cottage there." She pointed.

"Thank you."

She grinned again, mussed my hair, and padded away up the dock on bare feet.

~ * ~

"Chris," Mother called, "come here a second."

Everyone was gathered around the porch of the main building, grinning when I arrived.

"What is it?" I asked.

Glances passed from one person to another, from Mother's eyes, to Em's glasses to Leo's snaggle-toothed grin, to Tara's heavy-lidded smirk. Gazes filled with the power of knowledge withheld. They all knew something I didn't. A shared criticism of me or a punishment planned. The absolute reverse of a surprise birthday party.

"Something very exciting is happening," Father said. "A kind of a secret, I guess you could say. It's only been shared amongst us here. It has to do with a special invention."

"What kind of invention?"

Father looked at every face before returning his attention to mine.

"This is a big secret," he said. "You'll have to keep it just to yourself."

With all their eyes upon me, I said, "Yes. Okay."

"It's a time machine."

A strange feeling. I was surprised and let down at exactly the same moment. Surprised because I knew the strange force in my life had something to do with time, and it was about to be explained. Let down because there was something that rang exquisitely false about the words "time machine". I knew Dad was leaving something out. But, as always, I was prepared to take whatever was offered.

"Okay," I said, cautious as ever.

Uncle Leo held open the door, bicep rippling, and I followed Mother inside. Leo and Aunt Em's main cottage was a never-ending renovation project. Beginning as a single large room, it had burgeoned into a warren of weirdly proportioned hallways and unexpected doorways. Light and heat were unevenly distributed in the dwelling, so a shift from one area to another amounted to a total climate change. We wandered down a cold, damp hallway to a door held shut by a hook. Tara unfastened and pushed the door open.

A plain, windowless wooden room perhaps ten feet square. The walls seeped moisture and the floor reverberated as you stepped across it. It was obviously, a recent addition to the warren. In the center of the room sat a worn leather reclining chair, its bald spots patched by masking tape.

"Sit," Dad said.

I sat.

Dad and the others gathered around in a semi-circle. I closed my eyes, breathed in damp air, and pressed my lower back and legs into cool leather.

I thought of Peter.

"We're going to demonstrate this time machine for you," Father said. He paused, before adding, "Are you paying attention, Chris?"

My eyes sprang open: "Yes, I'm paying attention."

"Because if you're not interested in this, we'd be happy to leave you out of it..."

What I'm not interested in is being your guinea pig, I surprised myself by thinking. Of course, Father had me trained to keep such insurrections to myself.

"Sorry, dad. I'm listening."

"Pay attention. We're going to engage the Tipping mechanism and see how it works on you. You don't do anything. In fact, it's *critically* important you make no effort to do anything at all. Understood?"

"Understood."

"Because if you do, it won't work."

"Okay. And Tipping is...?"

"The word we've chosen for what the machine will do. That is, time travel. Any other questions?"

"No."

He turned to the group with a look that said, *we all know this is a joke, but I want you to keep quiet.*

Multiple sets of lips mashed together, stifling laughter.

"Close your eyes," Dad said.

I did. I breathed in deeply, filling my lungs with warm air. Then something...*happened* outside of me that pushed my attention to the far corners of the room. I discerned a faint ticking, like the tapping of bug claws, only magnified. *What the...?*

Suddenly, my body stiffened. I clenched my teeth, fighting it.

"Relax!" Father snapped.

I held rigid a moment or two before relaxing. My mind swum in the disorientation that accompanies held breath.

Something clicked in the back of my head. I felt my perceptive self flatten out, rise and then...*tip* over into....

What?

I opened my eyes.

Nothing had changed. Not a thing. The same ring of faces, the same smug smiles. The position of the chair exactly as it had been.

"Go outside and look," Dad said.

~ * ~

"And what did you see?"

Lu's question hovered in the mild dusk air. She sat, one leg curled under her, the other extended, a foot trailing in the water at the dock's edge.

"I saw..."

"It's okay, l'il man. Just go ahead and tell me. I'll believe ya."

"Okay." I glanced over my shoulder at the shoreline. I wasn't supposed to be visiting Lu (or, in fact, venturing off the property at all). But I had to speak to *someone.*

"Okay. First, I stood up and went down the hallway to the kitchen. That's when I noticed...the digital clock on the stove was blank, and the fridge wasn't humming."

Lu's eyes strayed to the dock as her hands found the guitar. A mournful chord sang in the air. She kept listening.

"There was something *different* about the air. From the way it had been before, and I have a hard time explaining it. But.... If you close your eyes and listen—I mean *really* listen—to the air, even up here in the country, you'll hear little sounds. Traffic. The noise of airplanes in the sky. Radio static. Power lines humming. The air is never really completely quiet. But after I came out of the Tipping Room and went through the kitchen, that's when I noticed…the air *was* quiet. For the first time *ever*. I couldn't hear *any* of those little things.

"So I went to the kitchen door and opened it and went onto the porch.

"Everything was *completely* different.

"First thing I noticed—there were no power lines. Like, there are these *poles*? At the edge of Uncle Leo's property that string this thick black cable up over the beach he keeps threatening to cut in *half. It wasn't there* anymore. I blinked to make sure it wasn't, like, an optical illusion or something. But no. It really wasn't there. And neither were any of the cottages across the lake. They were just *gone*. And in their place was forest.

"I stood there for ten whole minutes or more. And nothing moved. Nothing changed. I tried figuring out why things looked the way they did until it hit me. This was the way it must have been at the lake a hundred or more years ago. *Before* people settled here. It made sense. No planes, no cottages, no electric lines. Only the animals and forests would have been standing. I decided right then Father was telling the truth. There really *was* a Tipping Room with a time travel machine he'd invented. It explained everything.

"So I turned to go back in. And that's when I got *really* scared because *there was no house behind me*. I was standing in front of a doorway hanging in mid-air—not attached to anything—just hanging in space. Beyond it, I could see the stove and the kitchen chair and the big jar of spaghetti sauce on the shelf by the radio. But on either side of the door-shape there was nothing. The house didn't exist. And I knew if I reached out and shut that door, it would vanish, too, and I would be stranded in the past in the middle of nowhere."

I drew a deep breath.

"That's what happened."

Only then did it hit me how incredible my story sounded. *What if she doesn't believe me?* The possibility of being discounted as a liar by Lu terrified me beyond words.

"That's a really remarkable story. While you were telling it, I kept thinking, *oh, he's just a little boy. He's making it all up.* But those details—about the electricity and the air and the power lines and other properties being gone. Man!"

She picked her half-smoked joint from the tuning pegs and lit it.

"You're either a literary prodigy…or you're telling something that actually happened to you."

I waited.

"I believe you," she said at last.

"Lu, I love you."

She looked startled for a moment. "You're a total *sweetie!*" She smiled. "That's really nice. Thank you. But there's one problem with your story."

"There is?"

"Yeah. Think about it." Lu laid aside the guitar and hugged her knees to her chest. "When you started talking about this whole 'time travel' thing you and your alien parents are into, you mentioned the doctor's office. Where the walls quiver? Well, *he* wasn't in the Tipping Room. So how did he manage to achieve the same effect? Cause the walls to shimmer and distort and—presumably—displace the room in time the way you say your father is able to?"

"He must have a Tipping Mechanism in his office."

"But I thought your dad said it was a *new* invention."

I thought about that.

"And these two horrible little girls. What're they called? Terror and Hiss? I thought you said they played a game where they forced you to try and predict what was going to happen next. And little Hiss was always able to step behind a curtain or whatever and pop out with the right answer."

"So?"

"So where's her Tipping mechanism?"

I bit my lip.

"See, the problem is that I think these little creeps are able to do their thing with*out* a Tipping machine, or whatever it's called. If you and them are all the same and come from the same planet or place or wherever, then why do *you* have to go into a special room while *they* can just step behind a tree or whatever? It doesn't make any sense."

But Lu smiled at me as she finished.

"Don't worry, l'il man. We'll figure it out together."

She picked up her guitar, hugged me with one arm and started up the dock toward her house.

I heard a stone scuff on the beach behind us, and turned. Tara and Dis were standing in the trees at the edge of the water.

~ * ~

It wasn't the first time Father hit me. But it was the hardest.

"You little *bastard*!"

"Dad, I…"

"Chris, you *promised* to keep a secret, then *broke* that promise!"

"But, dad…"

His punch crushed the words in my mouth before they could form.

"We *trusted* you!"

Trust? The notion Father could have trusted me was a foreign concept. He might as well have been forecasting the weather in Chinese.

"Do you have any *idea* how sensitive the information we've shared with you is? And here I was thinking you were grown up enough to keep a secret. What I fool I am!"

He bent down, glaring into my eyes.

"You will never make a fool of me again."

I began to cry, disappointed in myself. But *I* was the fool. Fool for imagining losing his trust was worth mourning.

Father said because of my indiscretion, we had to leave in the morning. Until our departure, I was to stay out of everyone's way.

As he walked out, I spoke. "Dad…"

He turned.

There was so much I wanted to express: apologies, appeals for forgiveness, promises to reform. Mostly what I needed to share was my sense of regret. I believed I had lost something important. The words stumbled and caught in my mouth. I tried to speak but stuttered instead.

Father made a disgusted sound and marched out the door.

Dinner. While everybody gathered around the grill outside, I made a peanut butter sandwich in the kitchen. Ate it in my bedroom while finishing *Dune*.

Dusk. I walked the path through the forest to the lake, Lu's book under my arm. It was closer to night than it had ever been on any of my previous visits. Would she still be out? Would I be able to make my way back home in the dark? Wishing I'd brought a flashlight, I hurried to Lu's place.

A figure sat on the end of the dock, huddled in a blanket.

"Lu! I brought your book back."

She turned.

Same eyes, same hairstyle. But the slump of the shoulders, the caved chest, the age-lines tugging the mouth into a frown...

I slowed to a walk.

"Are you Lu's mom?"

The mouth curled into a sad smile.

"Hello, l'il man."

"*Lu?*"

"Your gal-pals came and paid me a visit." She pulled the blanket more closely around herself with gnarled fingers. "Told me I'd better watch my mouth or else..."

I trembled with rage. "Or else what?"

"They'd come and finish the job." Lu's eyelids clenched around remembered pain. "Those two horrible little girls came here, Chris, and they told me humans are forbidden to befriend your kind. They also told me you were handicapped—unable to do the same things as the others. So I was guilty of taking advantage of a cripple. That my spending time with you was a kind of abuse."

"No..."

"They told me I would have to be punished. So they did this to me."

Lu opened the blanket. In the fading light, I saw she was no longer clad in jeans and t-shirt but, instead wore a pair of old pajamas several sizes too big. Her arms and legs were spindly and scored with liver spots. Where once there had been healthy muscle and limbs was now bone and sagging flesh. And she exuded the vaguely sour odor of age.

"My God, Lu...I'm so—"

"Don't be sorry, l'il man. I'm glad I met and became friends with you. I'd do it again."

My eyes widened.

She reached out and squeezed my arm. "You're a sweet boy,

Chris. A lovely person. Good-hearted. You just have the bad fortune of being born into a terrible family. You're not the first. *But*. I doubt other kids in your position ever had to face abuse from parents who could time travel…"

"Abuse?"

"What else would you call the way they treat you? Now listen to the old lady." Lu grinned. "I love being able to say that, now, by the way…"

I fought back tears.

"You need to keep your wits about you, Chris. If little Terror and Hiss are any indication of what your people can do, then you'd better not upset them—particularly if you're somehow disadvantaged. Because they'll use that against you. Maybe try and hurt you the way they hurt me."

"What did they *do* to you?"

Lu was quiet for a moment.

"I was sitting here when they came out of the forest. Something about them, the way they moved so slowly and deliberately, told me I was in for it. They may just be little girls, but they're sinister, Chris. Vicious. Like a pair of little she-wolves. One came over and held up her hand. Just like this."

Lu showed me her palm.

"I felt my insides speed up. At first, it was like my heart was just beating faster. I started to run out of breath. And my chest hurt. Really bad. It felt like there was a machine in my body, jackhammering. It expanded until I felt something tear and a tightness crawled down my bones. I crawled to the side of the dock. I saw my reflection as I hung there over the water. My hair was white.

"I passed out. When I awoke, they were gone. And I…I looked like this."

It was like being told someone I'd hit with my car had died.

"Lu…"

"Listen, Chris. I'm going to tell you this; then I'm going to go inside. And you can never come back here. Not what I want, but the way things have to be. Understand?"

I nodded miserably.

"Good people can get extinguished if they stand next to someone who's evil for long enough. Your family, Chris, your people are fucking evil. You need to get away from them. Just as soon as you can. And as far *away* as you can. Before they destroy you. Because one day they will. Casually. Thoughtlessly. Just because they can.

"So keep your head down. Do as you're told. And start making plans to escape. First chance you get, go. It'll be lonely for a while. But sooner or later, you'll find people who understand you. But for now, you have to survive. That's a hell of a task for a little boy to have, but that's just the way it is. So hang in there. And don't forget me, Chris. Because I won't forget you. You take care, now."

I closed my eyes.

I couldn't bear to watch her leave.

CHAPTER FIVE
Rebellion

"Finished your math?"

"Yep."

"Go ahead throw it on my desk." Major Gordon settled himself behind the chess board in his office. "Shall we play before I jet home?"

The Major isn't exaggerating. Like many employees at Nellis FTC, he lives in Las Vegas, commuting back and forth to work each day on a chartered passenger jet out of McCarran International Airport which he jokingly calls *the bus*.

"When's the bus leaving today?" I ask.

"Ninety minutes. Should give us enough time for a quick game. Are you scheduled for another punch-up with Airman Ryerson this afternoon?"

"Yeah." I grin, cheek smarting as it folds around my newest black eye. I have been using the base library and what limited Internet access I have to read up on karate. Extra practice has enabled me to hold my own against her.

"She's starting to like you." Major Gordon conceals a pawn of each color in his fists. I tap the left. White. "Let me tell you she is beginning to demonstrate a grudging admiration for your guts. She says you have the makings of a real champ."

"I'm gonna' kick her ass one day."

"No lack of self-esteem there, I see." The Major replaces the pawns. "Airman Ryerson, frankly, scares the crap out of me...*and* half the officers on this base. The only person more frightening is the C.O. But not by much."

We settle into our game. Opening game is the most critical. Never allow the enemy to choose the battleground, I remind myself. By virtue of its pieces and their choreography, chess both creates and modifies the battleground with each new move. I push my King's pawn forward two squares. And think about Airman Ryerson.

"*I'm* not afraid of her," I declare.

"I can *see* that." Major Gordon mirrors my opening: Pawn to

King four. "You know, Chris, there are two types of bravery: the foolhardy bravery of the man who believes he's invincible—or who doesn't care if he lives—and the *measured* bravery of the man who lives to fight another day."

"What's the difference?" My Queen's Knight joins the fray.

"The first is the kind that starts wars. The second is the kind that wins them. You have to pick your battles carefully."

This makes sense to me. Major Gordon is an amazing teacher: one of those guys who turns every discussion—every problem—into a learning opportunity. I digest his comments before answering:

"So you're telling me I should be careful fighting Airman Ryerson."

"Well, that goes without saying. Look...you said you wanted to learn strategy. I've noticed the books you keep on your bedside table..."

"What about them?"

"Rommel's *Attacks*? *The Art of War*? You're a man on a mission, Chris. I can tell. I've seen it before. Men on missions can be extremely dangerous. To *themselves* more than anyone else."

He moves his Bishop.

"Meaning they don't live to fight another day?" I take his pawn with my Bishop.

Major Gordon points at the board. "Okay—that move, for instance. The one you just made."

"What's wrong with it? I ask. I just *captured* a pawn."

He holds my eyes for a long moment, smiling. Then he reaches out and sweeps my Bishop away with a pawn of his own.

"It was reckless. Losing a Bishop to a pawn? A waste. You're reading Sun Tzu, right? *The skillful general subdues his enemy without fighting*, Chris. That's what I mean about picking your battles. The same applies whether we're fighting in Medieval China or modern-day Vietnam. Or in a storeroom with Airman Ryerson."

"Thanks," I mumble, strangely embarrassed.

"Remember, it's better to wreck an enemy's *plans* than his army. Keep that in mind next time you go up against Ryerson. Or anybody."

~ * ~

Most of the things I know I've taught myself. Like karate, which I have to know in order to survive. Time travel is no different.

There are stories claiming the Aboriginal people of Australia must obey an occasional strong impulse to leave wherever they are and wander in the wilderness for a period. They call this "going walkabout" and if they do not yield to the impulse, they can sicken and die. I don't know if the stories are true or not. However, it is a reality for us. A Chronox—even a half-human one born here on Earth—must periodically enter the Discontinuity and travel the time streams. If not, he will sicken; like I did as a child. The doctor in the hazmat suit was right when he said Chronox parents teach their kids how to Tip into the Discontinuity. But this knowledge was kept from me. So like any kid, I used alternate means to discover what I wanted to know.

I began spying on my parents as well as Tara and Dis, alert for any behaviors that seemed unusual—non-human. Although the process of Tipping is mostly internal, there are a few external actions: closing the eyes, tilting the head back and to the left, raising the hands slightly from the sides. I began by imitating these actions. It took patience but the make-believe eventually paid off.

One afternoon, after a hundred attempts to Tip without lessons, I went through the motions and suddenly my mind calmed until I could discern a familiar faint ticking, like the claws of bugs at the edges of my consciousness. I recognized it as the same sounds I'd experienced in the Tipping Room. My body stiffened and something clicked in the back of my head. My perceptive self-flattened out, rose and then…

I didn't notice any results at first. But the next day, a few seconds before the ticking sound began, I heard the smash of glass breaking somewhere outdoors followed by a man's voice bellowing: "Esther, damn it!" I continued the process, feeling my flattened perspective rise and Tip. And then I heard the identical smash from before.

"*Esther, damn it!*"

I had succeeded in moving myself a few seconds backwards in time. I remember opening my eyes. And smiling.

Thus began my rebellion. It was a silent uprising, more like a guerilla war. I worked with my newfound ability in secret, never managing to displace myself in time more than fifteen seconds at most—and always into the past—but it was a start. I began a daily practice of Tipping, examining the shape and contours of the event itself, learning to discern the waves of the time-space continuum. I developed the ability to fold myself into a moment in time and remain there, invisible to anyone not actually traveling within the Discontinuity itself. At last I could Tip on my own, without the machine—news I kept to myself.

~ * ~

Fred escorts me to the medical clinic. He is different from the other guards. Where they tend to crowd me to remind me their job is to stop my running away, with Fred it's more like he is there to protect me. Perhaps the fact he is older has something to do with it.

"I have a son about your age," Fred told me once. "He's a nice kid, you'd like him."

The elevator door slides open. A medical attendant transporting a covered gurney nods to Fred.

"Hello, Chuck. How's your little girl?"

"Oh hey, Fred." Chuck glances uncomfortably at me, uneasy at chatting around a test subject. "Emily's fine. Out of the hospital yesterday."

"I'm glad she's been taken care of."

"Yes." Chuck follows Fred's gaze to the figure under the draped sheet. *Another failure*, he mouths. Fred nods, then glances at me and frowns. I pretend not to notice the conversation or the gurney or the fact the body under the sheet is about the right size to belong to a teenage boy or girl. The doors open and we step out onto carpet. Tara is confronting one of the doctors by the elevator doors.

"—won't accept another goddam failure. I thought you Army doctors were supposed to be *competent*!"

"It's not that simple, ma'am. It's—"

"Oh? Not that simple? Keeping people alive isn't simple? Gosh, I thought that was a doctor's *job*!"

I avoid Tara's eyes as we pass.

"The stresses on the body are considerable, even for a—"

"Oh? Imagine that! Going to university for eight years and getting paid a fortune to do a job that is *not…simple*!"

Fred and I turn down the corridor of examining rooms. I freeze.

The hallway is crammed with covered gurneys draped with sheets.

"Jesus..." Fred's hand drops to my shoulder. "C'mon, Chris. You don't need to see—"

"Ah! In the examining room please, guard!" The doctor, unwilling to risk standing up to Tara, instead raises his voice at Fred, who gives me a gentle nudge. An attendant comes and grabs one of the wheeled stretchers and pushes it toward the elevator as Fred opens the seal for me.

"Don't look, Chris," Fred murmurs. "Just find something in the room to fix your eyes on, okay? They're moving those stretchers out of here pretty fast so—"

"HOW HARD CAN IT BE?"

"It's—"

"YOU'RE INCOMPETENT!"

"No."

"YOU STUPID, STUPID FUCK!"

"Guard!"

Fred turns and moves toward the door. Tara has obviously gotten out of hand with the staff (as she has been known to do) and part of Fred's job is to maintain order in the Facility. That much is expected. But what amazes me is that he leaves the examining room door open without securing it behind him.

An attendant comes and removes another gurney.

I wait until Fred has turned the corner. I find a gurney and slip under the sheet beside the cold, naked body of a dead boy about my age. I lie very still. It doesn't take long for an attendant to come and wheel us away.

~ * ~

The elevator rises to ground level. I hear engines and voices, and gag on exhaust fumes. When the attendant leaves I lift the sheet just far enough to peek out. My gurney has joined two dozen others crowding the loading dock of a garage. A group of enlisted men are pulling the bodies from the gurneys and tossing them into the backs of the trucks under the supervision of a female sergeant. I am waiting for an opportune moment to slip out when a better idea occurs to me.

My gurney is pushed forward. The sheet is ripped off. I lay still as hands grasp my wrists and ankles. I am swung back and forth a few times before being launched through the air to land on a heap of bodies in the bed of a truck. The dead shrink and stiffen until they are all protruding hip bones and sharp elbows, so the landing is like being tossed onto piled bracken. I wince but remain still even as other bodies fall on me.

Soon the back flap closes, and the truck pulls away from the loading dock. I open my eyelids to slits. No guard. For a cargo of dead people, why would there be? I wriggle out from under the bodies and peek out the flap. The truck is snaking down one of the winding dirt roads that connects the Facility to the outer edges of Nellis, passing through large stretches of open desert—vast, undeveloped sectors of the base. When the driver slows to take a curve, I hop down. I land hard and tear the right knee of my jeans.

I am in a moonscape—a parched and desolate wasteland of sand and shattered rock where only sunburn and scorpions crawl. I stand, breath crushed from my lungs by the heat. I squint. A silver thread crawls out of the brown tangle of rock and cactus and I recognize the steel glimmer of the base fence-line. In a daze I hike to intercept it. I follow, knowing sooner or later it will pass close by a road.

After an hour I hear the base alarm. *So they know I'm gone.* I put my head down and continue trudging. Topping a rise, I note the curve of highway that bends inward toward the fence at the foot of the hill.

A man is there. It's dark, but the moon is bright and washing everything in silver light. Even from a distance I can see the ponytail, the Bermuda shorts and recognize the wide stance of his combat boots in the universally recognizable posture. A woman sits in a parked SUV, looking amused as he finishes. I lurch into a stumbling run.

"Hey, mister!"

He zips up and turns to me. "Hey, ah, look," he says gruffly, "I'm sorry about…you-know-what. But man when you gotta go, you gotta—"

"Help me? Please?"

Something in the man's sudden stillness draws the attention of the woman in the SUV. Their eyes meet briefly. When he looks back at me, all gruffness is gone. Not sure what he does for a living, but I'm thinking a teacher or a cop or a firefighter because he is sudden alertness and burning concern that cuts through layers of intervening chit-chat. "What's wrong? Are you in trouble?"

"Yes. I'm—this is the base. Nellis. Area 51? Yeah. I'm inside. I'm a prisoner. And they're experimenting on me and a whole bunch of others."

"The military?"

"Yeah."

The man stares at me hard for a long moment. "Wait here."

He marches to his SUV, speaks briefly to the women behind the wheel then pulls a battery charger from a side storage panel.

"One thing I learned in Iraq," he says, clipping one of the cable clamps to the fence mesh, "is how to short out an electric fence. Take ten steps back for me, would ya?"

I turn and begin pacing away from the fence-line, counting my steps. By the time I reach four, the air is filled with the rising scream of engines. I spin around. A county sheriff and an Air Force security officer have blocked in the SUV and are advancing toward it. The deputy and the air cop both stop, draw and level their guns.

There is not a word of warning, no command for the driver to get out with her hands up. The two lawmen just immediately begin shredding the van with gunfire. The windshield and passenger windows disintegrate like the walls of a fish-tank imploding and the woman inside jerks like a ragdoll shaken back and forth in the mouth of a dog. Smoke, as from burning bone, clouds the wrecked interior and blood mists the jagged edges of the shattered glassware. And still the firing continues.

That's when the man with the ponytail does something insane. He drops the battery charger, puts his head down and rushes the deputy, running head-first into the gunfire. I keep expecting him to be stopped and spun to the ground by a stray bullet, but it doesn't happen. The man hits the deputy and slams him up against the hood of his car. The cop jerks and twists, pinned, working to get the business end of his sidearm between himself but before he can the ponytailed man reaches out with clawed fingers and—

My god.

There is a loud popping noise then a spray of blood and suddenly the ponytailed man is loping toward the open door of the sheriff's cruiser, a hamburger-sized chunk of throat-meat dangling from his right hand.

"Stop!" screams the air cop.

Ponytail throws the bloody flesh to the ground, jumps behind the wheel of the deputy's cruiser, and hits the ignition. Moments later, the stolen car is out of range and speeding down the highway.

The smoke and blood from the wrecked SUV settles to silence.

Sirens split the air.

The security forces officer jerks his gun toward me and screams: "You! Get down! Get down on the fucking ground! Right now!"

I do what he says.

CHAPTER SIX
Nineteen-Sixty-Something

"...then killed the sheriff's deputy and escaped in his vehicle. A BOLO alert has been issued to state and federal law enforcement for this sector and the Department of Homeland Security has been advised. Our operatives are hunting him. He won't last long out there."

The security forces colonel finishes his report and closes the folder. The guy is career military, so he has no problem standing at attention there in the shadowed half-light of my father's office. Major Gordon on the other hand does have a problem doing that, and fidgets slightly, his eyes shifting back and forth between Father and myself.

"Colonel Parker," my father says finally, "what is the likelihood of containment?"

"High. We'll get him. And if he blabs any of what Chris said, he'll be dismissed as another conspiracy fruitcake. Dreamland has endured much worse."

My father leans forward, sifting through thoughts, arranging ideas in his mind the way he does. He has this way of measuring words carefully, like a carpenter fitting boards, gauging the fit of half-truth to half-truth for continuation of the sprawling architecture.

"I'll speak to my son alone now, please."

"Sir." Parker stiffens to attention then leaves. Major Gordon lingers a second or two longer, trying to catch my gaze but is unsuccessful. After a few lost seconds, he turns to go.

The door closes softly somewhere in the shadowed darkness.

"So you've made a second escape attempt." Father's voice is modulated. Soft. "It has resulted in the death of two people and a leak about the nature of the project here. You've jeopardized everything I have spent the last twenty years working for.

"You are no longer my son and completely unworthy of trust. You're a—"

Words leap from my mouth like a burning coal. "*When the hell have you ever shown me any trust?*"

After a brief silence, Father says, "Okay." And, pushing back from the desk, continues, "I see there's no reasoning with you. I've tried extending a hand and you've bitten it. You can't be treated like a mature individual and now, because of this latest breach of *trust*—"

Leaning on the word as he smiles at me.

"—you know too much. You're…frankly? Can I be frank? You're a danger to the project. You're going to be put in time out, Chris, until this is over. This hurts me more than it will hurt you, but it's for your own good. Understand?"

I sit stone-faced, determined to deny him the satisfaction of a reply.

~ * ~

Tara adjusts her hair in the rear-view mirror. Her eyes flick toward me briefly before returning to the road. Soon we are on the highway, bearing for the cottage.

At age sixteen, Tara's taste in clothing and fashion ran toward the conservative, giving her the appearance of a teenage CEO. Just a while ago we were about the same age. Now she spears me with the domineering judgmental glare of a full adult. I shrink a little further into the back seat and try hard not to show how deeply she can wound me with a glance.

"Dis. What time are we due back for Jared's party?"

"Six," Dis replies from the passenger seat.

"So showing up by eight is fine," Tara says with a sigh. "You won't give me any trouble will you now, Chris?"

I remember the way she hurled me into the past as a child, certain her power has grown considerably since then. So, I swallow and say nothing.

"Know what the problem with you is, Chris? You're *immature*."

Enclosed by doubt and fear, I say nothing.

"It's a shame, you know." Tara's attention drifts out the driver's side window. "You could have been a good friend for us. Despite the age difference. But that's impossible now. It's sad! You just never …*grew up*."

Ashamed, I say nothing.

"It's your own fault, really. There's so much we could have offered you. But you *had* to be selfish and antisocial. Are you *happy* now, Chris?"

I say nothing.

"Stupid, stupid, stupid Chris," she says chuckling.

We take an off-ramp onto a two-lane road winding into the trees. The smell of approaching spring is stronger here. I live in that scent, positioning myself to absorb the small stream of it as it comes in the open window. *Here* at least is something living—something I can give myself to. I try to convince myself that I'm not afraid as we turn down a familiar dirt road. The roof of Uncle Leo's cottage pokes up over the tree-tops, growing larger as we creep closer.

Tara parks beside the beach with its dangling power line. A half-dozen folded lawn chairs are stacked beside the faded wooden dock. The dishrag still hangs from the wash line by a single corner. A cold gust shakes the leaves of the nearest maple. When it subsides a stillness falls so completely it's as if the world has died.

"Let's get this over with," Tara says.

We march across the snow-faded lawn to the wooden porch and mount the steps. Tara wears the key Father gave her on a string around her neck and uses it to unlock the cottage door. We pass through the silent kitchen and hallway to the padlock securing the room that holds the Tipping Machine. Tara unlocks it and the door swings open in a blast of moldy damp.

"Sit down, Chris."

I cross the floor on trembling legs and slide over the arm of the patched recliner and into the seat.

Tara bends to the computer equipment. "This is going to hurt us more than it's going to hurt you, Chris," she insists in an echo of Father's words. "Isn't that right, Dis?"

"Right, Tara."

"We've made arrangements for you to stay with some people," Tara continues. "They have no idea, really, who we are or that we're from another time. And I seriously doubt they'd even believe you if you said anything. But stay with them for a few days and don't cause any trouble. Understand? Or else…"

"Or else *what*?" I demand, brave because I'd soon be free of her.

Tara's smile is a flash of sun on ice.

"I remember a certain girl you once liked, Chris. Used to play guitar?"

A ripple passes through me like an old t-shirt being ripped. I am so sick—so *tired*—of fighting and losing and being hurt all the time. I want to close my eyes and go away. Just fall asleep and keep on sleeping 'til I die. My tired mind resonates with the single word...*Lu*.

"I hate you, Tara," I whisper. "God, I hate you so much I want to *kill* you..."

"I'm sorry you feel that way. Maybe, once you've grown up, you'll..."

But by then I've stopped listening altogether. The disorientation, the ticking at the edges of my consciousness, the sense of falling from a great height: all these things occur. And then quite suddenly...I am alone in the room.

Strange, I think.

The room itself has never changed like this before. I open my eyes to a version of the room that is distinctly different. For one thing, it is freshly cleaned, dusted, and swept as if awaiting presentation by a real estate agent.

For another (and perhaps more alarming), all the computer equipment is gone.

Some great change is happening. I can sense it the way you feel the thump of furniture moving in the place next door. A great migration across multiple dimensions at once, like the rotation of planets around a star. The past, the present—wherever that now was—and the future are all in play. And I am sitting in this chair in an abandoned house, disconnected from everything but feeling it all around me.

I rise unsteadily and move through the house toward the kitchen.

The kitchen is different. It is colder and suddenly more spacious where chairs are absent, and objects have been removed from shelves. From the great spaces where the stove and refrigerator once stood comes a draft smelling faintly of turpentine and mouse turds. Floating shafts of dust fill the air. The quality of light coming in through the window is different. I step over and push the curtain aside. I am peering through the window into a hallway.

So we're indoors all of a sudden...

I turn the knob and step out.

The floor beyond is bare concrete strewn with bits of trash and old newspapers. The corridor, lit by dangling bulbs hung every dozen feet, recedes into darkness at either end. Numbered doors that haven't seen a coat of paint in years line the walls. I turn. I step into the apartment hallway. Turning back, I can still see the empty kitchen of Uncle Leo's cottage through the doorway behind me.

"...should just be for a day or two. You're sure this will be enough money?" I hear Tara's voice, followed by a man's, low and melodious.

"Oh, yeah. Gosh, I mean—this is almost *too* generous. We're just happy to help out."

I glance around. The apartment next door is open. Tara stands in the doorway talking to a barefoot man holding a guitar and balancing a puzzled expression on his bearded face.

"Here he is." Tara turns and gives me her best plastic smile. "Come *here*, little cousin! Don't be afraid. Now...Chris? This is Theodore. He and his nice sister Laura will be taking care of you for a couple of days. Would you like that?"

Frowning at the stupidity of the last question, I say hi to Theodore.

Theodore flashes a grin that is all beard and teeth. "Peace, Chris. Nice to meet ya'. Uh, hey, I gotta' take care of something in the kitchen. I'll be..."

Right back. The words hang unspoken in the dark air as he pads down the hallway past a woman who is almost an identical copy of himself (although shorter, female, and beardless). She wears a knee-length cotton dress and stands wiping her hands on a dish rag, the toes of one dirty foot wedged against the ankle of the other. Her expression is difficult to read. But her eyes glimmer as she leans against the wall, head cocked to one side, noticing every detail of events unfolding before her.

"You take care now, Chris," Tara says in a stage voice. "Oh, I'm going to *miss* you!"

She hugs me, one-armed, and I pretend to hug back. *She must have gotten here ahead of me*, I think. *Didn't need the Tipping Room. Just went ahead and...*

Tara steps into the apartment from which I emerged, pulls the door closed behind her and vanishes.

The barefoot woman and I stare at each other in silence. Then she finishes wiping her hands and shakes her head, a slow smile creasing her thin face.

"I'm Laura," she says. "Chris, I got to say; I think your cousin is probably the biggest goddam phony I've ever met."

I blink.

"How would you like a brownie and a nice big glass of cold milk?"

I like Laura.

~ * ~

There are a half-dozen plants in little clay pots on the window-sill. Hand-stitched pillows huddle around a low table on the living-room floor in place of chairs. There are plank-and-brick bookshelves crammed with used paperbacks and blankets and wall-hangings in muted blues and browns, all hand-made. It takes me a moment to recognize there is no TV. The only concession to modern comforts is a portable turntable on the floor beside two milk-crates crammed with LPs. I bend to examine these.

"Uh, Chris?"

Laura is smiling.

"We leave our shoes by the door here, 'kay?"

"Sorry." I kick off my sneakers and carry them to a place by the door beside a set of stout work-boots that could only be Theodore's. Next to these are a pair of flip-flops in Laura's size, and an identical pair in a child's size. Beside them is a coat closet with its door removed. A sting grocery bag hangs on a hook inside beside a tiny shelf supporting three glass Coke bottles into which are jammed sickly yellow candles. Black-out insurance, I guess. I hike to the kitchen in my stocking feet.

Laura is knifing generous brownies from a baking pan that has seen better days. Because there is no kitchen table, I find a clear space on the counter to sit, legs dangling over the edge.

"How old are you, Chris?"

"Fifteen."

Laura smirks. "But they treat you like you're eight. Is your dad a businessman or something?"

"Yeah. He, uh..."

"Tell me something you believe is true."

"Huh?"

Laura turns to me, knife blade sheathed in brownie goo. "Go on, Chris. Tell me one thing you believe to be true."

I think long and carefully before replying. And feel an uncomfortable twinge as I say, "The strong destroy the weak. That's Nature's way."

Laura puts the last brownie next to three others on a plate and sets down the knife.

"Do you really believe that or is that just something your Dad says?"

"I…I don't know."

She nods slowly. "You wanna' know what I think?" she says after a minute. "I think you don't really believe that. I think you just say it because it's something your father believes, and he's trying to get you to agree. But I think you know it's bullshit because you're smarter than he is. And a hell of a lot nicer."

I grin.

Now I *really* like Laura.

"Grab me those glasses, will ya'?"

I gather the four glasses on the countertop and follow her out to the living room. Theodore sits on one of the cushions beside the low table, tuning his guitar contemplatively. He does not look up until Laura speaks.

"Chris's father believes it's natural for the strong to destroy the weak."

The edge of Theodore's beard shifts upwards in a smirk. "Sounds a lot like our dad." His hand drops from the fret board to the table. "Remember how he used to talk about MacArthur?"

"Was your father in the war, Chris?" Laura raises her eyebrows with the question as she pours glasses of milk.

I recall my mothers' tales of orange skies and detonating bombs.

"Yes. He and mom were refugees. Their home got attacked."

"And they came here?" Theodore puts aside his guitar. "Your folks are immigrants?"

"Yeah."

"From where?"

"Oh, uh…. You couldn't pronounce it."

Laura and Theodore exchange a glance. They seem dissatisfied with this answer so I shove a wedge of brownie into my mouth and start chewing before they can ask a follow-up question. I chew and think. Hard. Tara's warning to keep my mouth shut hovers in my mind. Meanwhile, I have no idea where I am and even less an idea of *when*. The lack of furnishings makes it difficult to judge. A TV, its make and model suggesting a date of manufacture, might help. I can't very well *ask* where we are without appearing even more confused than I already feel. So I just focus on how happy the food makes me and the vast lack of tension I feel in their company. So different from home. Laura and Theodore aren't *expecting* anything of me, so they can't be disappointed. It is a nice change of pace.

"Chris, do you have any brothers or sisters?" Laura asks as a little girl of about five, barefoot like Laura and Theodore, her tummy and chest covered in chaotic swatches of paint, comes into the room. The matching mess on the back of her knuckles and right forefinger suggest she has an artistic streak.

"No brothers or sisters," I reply. I look at the little girl. "Hi. What's your name?"

She considers me gravely, apparently feeling no pressure to reply right away. Theodore and Laura, I notice, do not push her to speak but instead wait patiently for her to answer in her own good time.

"Sunshine," the little girl says finally. "My name is Sunshine."

"That's a very nice name," I tell her. I look at Laura. "Is she your daughter?"

"Laura is my aunt," Sunshine says. Then she grins and trots over to Theodore, who takes Sunshine in his arms as she curls up on his lap like a blonde, paint-spattered kitten.

"Sunshine is my little girl," he says, kissing the top of her head.

"Where's her mom?" I ask.

Theodore shrugs.

"Theo's mate gave birth to Sunshine when we were living on a commune in Taos" Laura says. "She took off a few days later—nobody knows where. We're Sunshine's family, now."

"Family," Sunshine chuckles.

"But no mom?" I ask. "That doesn't seem—"

I stop myself in the instant before saying *right*. Laura just shrugs. And Theodore runs his hands over Sunshine's long hair, smiling softly.

"We believe," he says gently, "a family is whatever you make it. And that—ultimately—you choose your own."

~ * ~

I sleep in a nest of pillows and blankets fashioned for me in the living room. I wake twice during the night—once to quench my thirst with a stream of water from the kitchen faucet and then later in the very early morning. I am deep into a dream about dolphins when a sound—kind of a high-pitched squeak intrudes. Unable to place it within the underwater setting, I come awake in slow, fuzzy stages. It takes me a moment or two to recognize the noise is from the street. Curious, I crawl to the window and peer out.

The street Theodore and Laura live on is as narrow and trash strewn as the hallway outside their apartment door. The high, rounded curbs pack in the narrow thoroughfare and massive iron streetlamps dangle over the sidewalks. Sunrise is just beginning to peek through the high-rises to the east, but daylight hasn't found its way down through the roof-tops yet. The squeak is approaching the far corner of the street, a high-pitched repetitive *kree…kree…kree*. When its source appears, I am taken completely by surprise.

The squeak emanates from a crooked bicycle wheel attached to a large wooden…what? The word "contraption" springs to mind. It's a large wooden cart or wagon, four panels enclosing a large oxygen bottle below a whimsical roof with shingles and gables resembling those of a Swiss mountain cottage. The wagon is pushed along by a thick and fat solid man who wears what appears to be some sort of costume, similar to the old milkman uniform: ice-cream-colored slacks and dress shirt, black shoes and belt and a skinny black tie hanging down from around the neck. His face above the tight collar is fleshy and expressionless, with tiny little lips and piggy eyes peering out from folds of flesh. A huge man moving quietly through the pre-dawn streets.

He reaches the corner of Laura's and Theodore's street and turns down it, taking the sidewalk past our stoop. *Kree…kree…kree.* The sound of the bent tire grows louder as it approaches. The gabled roof of the cart with its oxygen (*must be helium*) bottle approaches and I can see writing in curlicue script tucked below the roof gables:

PHIL'S BALLOONS - 5¢

Kree…kree…kree.

The cart draws level with our stoop. The huge man stops

directly below our window and looks up at me.

How he knows I am here, tucked below the sill and partially concealed by curtains, is a mystery. But he stares right at me and his ugly, meaty face lights up in the sweetest smile. As I watch, he produces an unfilled balloon—a red one—from his pocket and fits it to the mouth of the helium tank. With a twist of the wheel, the red skin fills. Once it is completely inflated, he yanks it free and ties it with a swift skilled flurry of fingers. Smiling at me, he releases it to rise up past the stoops and windows and roofs of the tenements to disappear into the cloudy pre-dawn sky. Then, with a nod, he turns back to his cart and continues squeaking up the street. When he reaches the far intersection, he turns the corner. And disappears.

~ * ~

A few hours later I am awakened by a hammering on the apartment door. I find my feet and stumble over. Struggling with the lock, I hear movement in the hallway behind me. Laura's approaching, holding a blanket up to her body. I open the door.

A man in a tie-dye t-shirt and shorts stands scrubbing the underside of his beard with the fingernails of one hand while peering up the hallway toward something.

"Yogi Joe!" Laura cries, dropping the blanket to her feet and rushing to enfold the newcomer in a hug. I don't realize she is naked until she has him in her arms. The man smiles and hugs Laura back, humming in satisfaction. I pick up the blanket, ready to hand it to back, embarrassed by Laura's nakedness. I am apparently alone in this.

"You're too short to be Theodore," the man called Yogi Joe says as he releases her and turns to me. "Unless, of course, you're a younger version of Theodore who's somehow managed to travel forward in time…"

"Could be," I dead-pan. "Depends what year it is."

Yogi Joe's eyes widen in his hairy face and he roars with laughter. His hands come together in a prayer-like gesture below his chin. "I'm Joe. Who are you, young time traveler?"

"Chris," I say, returning his gesture.

"Chris is staying with us while his cousin is out of town." Laura's hand squeezes my shoulder as she takes the blanket back and drags it around her torso. "Chris, this is Yogi Joe, a friend from the commune. Joe, how did you *find* us?"

Yogi Joe steps crisply into the apartment and closes the door behind him. "Your last letter had a routing stamp," he explains, following Laura into the living room. "I just showed up downtown and started asking around."

"You came here from *Taos*?" I ask, scanning Yogi Joe from the top of his crew-cut head to the soles of his travel-worn sandals. "Where's your luggage?"

Yogi Joe holds out his arms. "I'm wearing it," he says, and laughs again.

"Yogi Joe is a *sannyasi*," Laura explains as we make breakfast and Yogi Joe showers. "He lives without possessions."

"Like a priest?"

"Kind of. Seeing me naked really embarrassed you, didn't it?"

"Kind of."

Laura naked was actually beautiful. And somehow that bothered me immensely.

"Poor Chris. So uptight. We're going to have to help you loosen up." She hugs me with one arm and scrambles eggs with the other.

~ * ~

I'm usually awkward around people I've just met for the first time. But for some reason, strolling toward the center of town later that morning to attend a street fair with the group, I feel really comfortable.

"So Chris!" Yogi Joe walks on one side of me and Theodore on the other. "Goin' to school, man?"

"Uh, yeah," I say, sorting through possible answers in the event he asks *which* school. But it turns out I don't have to worry. Yogi Joe is a big-picture kind of guy.

"Do you like school?" Theodore asks.

"No."

He and Theodore grin at exactly the same moment.

"A dumb question to ask a fifteen-year-old," Theodore admits cheerfully.

"If you weren't in school, what would you be doing with your time?" Yogi Joe asks seriously.

The license plates of the passing cars say State of Washington: first clue to my whereabouts.

"If I wasn't in school right now, I would be spending time finding out about myself. Who I *am*. Who my *family* is. There's so much that's been kept from me and so little that I know and so much that I *want* to learn. School just seems to clutter up my head with facts that distract me from knowing myself. I mean…how can I live *well* if I don't even know who I *am*?"

Yogi Joe remains silent throughout this even as the crowd thickens around us and I have to raise my voice to finish my statement audibly. Suddenly, there are people *everywhere*: individuals, families, small groups of friends, young and old in bright colors and sandals with long hair and t-shirts adorned with peace signs and doves in chaotic blurs of mismatched color. I see a flash of motion as jugglers work and the lumbering progress of street performers hobbling past on stilts and people holding banners demanding clean water or peace or respect for the Earth. Music fills the air, tumbling from the bongos and guitars of impromptu jam bands forming on the sidewalk to compete with the tinny, one-dimensional threads of sound issuing from shop-front speakers. Stores and boutiques crowd in, doors ajar to release a glimpse of wares or owners standing expectantly at the threshold, wreathed in clouds of incense.

In answer to my response Yogi Joe only says, "Wow."

The crowd thins where the sidewalk broadens at the mouth of an alley.

Laura pauses.

Light spears down to touch a section of wall in the alley beside a newspaper dispenser. Laura stares intently at this golden patch, squinting as she cranes toward it. She jumps when I touch her shoulder.

"Laura?"

Her eyes widen on me. She stares at me, then back to the patch of sunlight in the alley. Then back at me. Then blinks twice and shakes her head.

"What's the matter?"

"Nothing," she says a little too loudly, then grabs Sunshine's hand and walks away quickly.

I glance at the top paper in the dispenser's rack.

SEATTLE POST-INTELLIGENCER
Saturday, May 17th, 1969

The crowd dribbles onto a crosswalk that terminates at a set of wooden traffic barriers manned by an overweight, indolent cop. Several city blocks, cordoned off to make space, comprise the heart of the street fair. I sense a shift in energy the moment we enter the labyrinth: the absence of automobiles, of ordered pedestrian traffic and the number of hippies magically transforming the zone into a quasi-Medieval village in the midst of downtown Seattle. I see a sign advertising vegetarian tacos, a man in a top hat balancing on a unicycle, a laughing girl with flowers in her hair…

"Ever been to one of these?" Theodore asks.

"No. It's cool!"

Yogi Joe stops beside a group of orange-robed Hare Krishnas he apparently knows and strikes up a conversation. I drift ahead alone, losing myself in the sights and sounds. A bearded man in an army fatigue jacket strums a guitar under a tree. A few meters further along, a mime is blowing up pantomime balloons for a crowd of children, Sunshine among them.

I smile.

I have so *many* problems (my parents, the present displacement in time, the Project, and the experiments at the Facility), but suddenly none of them matter. I am *here*, absorbed in a vibrant world crowded with people intent on creating…*fun*. Fun is something I know very little about. The more I wander the packed streets, passing booths and strolling minstrels and brightly dressed people having their faces painted or their hair braided, or their fortunes read, the less isolated I feel.

A half-hour passes.

The fair crosses another intersection, this one blocked on all four approaches. At its center, a group of street performers enact a play involving a skeleton dressed as Uncle Sam. I drift through. Duck among the booths on the far side. The smells of frying food, burning sweet-grass, and a dissipating cloud of marijuana smoke all linger in the air. A group of girls in peasant dresses stand in a tight circle, giggling. The line of shop fronts to my left breaks abruptly to become a park.

Yogi Joe, along with a few Hare Krishnas and a group of other folks, are sitting in a circle on the lawn. Yogi Joe scoots aside to made room for me.

"The word *yoga*," he is saying, "means 'union,' okay? So if we're talking yoga exercises or yoga-meditation, we're not talking about something exotic or weird: we're just talking about uniting the different parts of ourselves into a functioning whole. Like my friend Chris here asks—"

His hand descends onto my shoulder.

"—how can we live effectively if we don't know who we are? I mean, *it's a great question*. From a guy who's…how old are you, Chris?"

"Fifteen," I say, ears reddening, embarrassed by the sudden attention.

"Pretty heavy wisdom for fifteen, right? *I* thought so, anyway."

Smiles and some light applause and affirmations of *right on!* drift around the circle. I want to beam, to bathe in this glow of approval and return it in kind. But I am still too traumatized to extend myself emotionally. I keep my head down.

"Close your eyes," Yogi Joe tells everyone.

We do.

He makes us wait for the sound of his voice. And when it comes, traveling through eye-dark to a place very deep inside, it touches down very gently:

"Sit. With your spine straight, but your neck and shoulders …relaxed. This is *pos*sible if you aren't…tense. Good. Now. Breathe. Easily."

A long pause.

"Feel it?"

Another pause.

"Your tongue sits on the floor of your mouth. Re…*laxed*. That's good. And your attention…is directed to…the in*side* of your forehead."

I feel something jolt loose deep inside me as if unclenching: a fist opening to the sky.

Yogi Joe's voice continues to come from very far away, telling us to say a word inside our minds—to repeat it softly to ourselves. And then he gave us the word. I examine its contours by turning it this way and that—*not* probing for weakness—before beginning the process of repetition, over and over again within my own mind…

~ * ~

Meditation changes *everything*.

I pace the crowded streets alone, attuned to brightness. The world is *new* again, as if the entire thing has been scrubbed with light. Thoughts come in an ordered stream as opposed to a disorganized blur. And instead of the scrambled sensation inside my chest, a kind of lightness...

At peace with myself.

The crowd thins. Dusk is falling. I find a quiet alleyway and enter, following the wall toward a clean spot beside a newspaper dispenser. Sink down cross-legged. Close my eyes.

Meditation.

I compose my mind, sitting as instructed, and begin repeating Yogi Joe's special word. Joy crawls like carbonated liquid up my spine to explode inside my brain. I let go an involuntary gasp. My head swims—not in disorientation, but a kind of laser-like clarity knitting everything together. I feel the disconnection inside me melt away to embrace the presence of the world beyond in...harmony.

Union.

I am too absorbed in all of this to notice the sensation of falling, or the ticking noise at the far edge of my consciousness until long after it has begun.

Open. Your. Eyes.

I do.

Laura at the mouth of the alley, squinting in my direction. And someone stepping up behind her, someone both weirdly familiar and intimately foreign. I am still sorting through faces in my mind when it suddenly occurs to me—

That's me!

A weird throbbing echoes in my ears; the angle of the *sun* has changed! It was somehow *morning* again...and...

I am seeing *myself.*

Laura jumps and turns toward the other me when he touches her shoulder. I see her mouth the word *nothing* before grabbing Sunshine's hand and walking away quickly.

I meet my own gaze. And, in the instant before dissolving back into the present, I blink.

CHAPTER SEVEN
Theft

I can time travel.

I am cross-legged on the living-room floor, picking at chords on Theodore's guitar. I have no natural musical talent but toying with the instrument is something I've done on and off as a sort of tribute to Lu. It calms me. Mostly. Although right now I'm having a difficult time sitting still because; *I can time travel.*

Courtesy of Yogi Joe's meditation instruction, I have transcended my fifteen second limit. I can now displace myself up to a day either forward or backward in time. Turns out I'm not "handicapped" or "stupid" at all. With continued practice I might expand my capabilities even further. It's a critical step in my freedom and in my campaign against Father and the Project.

Of course, I am up against a far superior force. In addition to the might of the U.S. military, I face Tara and Father and a whole group of other Chronox able to move effortlessly through time without the slightest limitation. Hopeless, perhaps. But I'm learning about a little war currently underway in this When—one pitting a small, backwards nation against the largest military on Earth. And the small backwards nation—a place called Vietnam—is winning.

Spread out on the floor is a newspaper article about the latest setbacks. It seems the Viet Cong, being generally shorter and smaller than Americans, are able offset their enemy's technological superiority and equalize the balance of power by using an extensive network of tunnels to hide their movements and gain tactical advantage. An ingenious solution to a difficult problem. The essence of warfare is the intelligent application of force. Martial arts teach us how a smaller, weaker opponent can overcome a larger one by combining will and technique. I turn these ideas over in my mind as I strum chords.

Tunnels…equalizing the balance of power…large against small…intelligent application of force…deception and maneuver. And; *I can time travel.*

~ * ~

The strange balloon man reappears later that morning. I am flipping through Theodore's collection of vinyl record albums when the *kree…kree* of his cart sounds from outside. Sunshine appears and goes immediately to the window.

"That balloon man is back!" She does a little happy dance. "Laura, look!"

Laura appears in the kitchen doorway, wiping her hands on a dish towel. "You wanna' balloon, Sunshine?" She digs in a pocket of her dress. "Here's a nickel. I'll take you down. Or…maybe Chris?"

"Sure! C'mon Sunshine." I hold out my hand. The little girl grasps it with an eager smile, and we head out the door and down the steps to the sidewalk. A small cluster of children has formed around the now stationary cart. The balloon man (Phil?) is blowing up balloons and tying them to strings. As we approach, he speaks to a small black boy with a handful of pennies.

"Of course, Otis," Phil says quietly. "Now what color would you like?"

"Green!" Otis, grinning, is obviously excited. He watches as Phil carefully produces a green balloon from his pocket and fills it with a flourish from the helium tank. He ties a string around it and hands it to Otis with infinite gentleness.

"There you go, Otis. That'll be five cents please."

"Here!" Otis thrusts out his fist.

"Thank you, sir." Phil takes the money and offers a small salute. "A pleasure doing business with you."

Otis wanders off, delighted.

We await our turn, gradually moving closer to Phil, who works carefully and unhurriedly, filling balloons and tying them to strings and offering them to children as if it is the most important job in the world.

Why not? I think as we draw closer. *Why couldn't being the balloon man be the most important job on Earth?*

At last it is our turn.

"Well hello, Sunshine." Phil smiles at her. "Do you want your usual?"

"Yes please!"

Phil produces a long thin white balloon which he fills partway before grasping the skin in thick fingers and beginning to twist it against itself. Under his manipulations, the balloon transforms itself into a long, thin dog which hovers in the air before Sunshine's amazed eyes. Phil ties the rope to the finished balloon sculpture around its doggy neck like a leash.

"There you go, Sunshine. I know you're not allowed to have a *real* dog. But you know I keep Barky safe for you here." He pats his helium tank. "And, you can have him whenever you like."

"Thank you, Phil!"

I hand over the nickel Laura gave me. Phil takes it and examines me carefully.

"You don't belong here, do you? You're like me." He smiles. "We're both like these balloons. Deflated. Until someone fills us, helps us grow to reach the right size, we'll never fly."

Before I can ask him what he means, he turns and pushes his cart away up the sidewalk.

~ * ~

I've only known Yogi Joe for about twenty-four hours, but I already trust him. So when he volunteers to run to the corner market to pick up vegetables I ask if I can tag along. "I want to ask you some questions," I say.

"Ask away, Chris!" We hike the trash-strewn hallway to the stairwell. Joe's flip-flops slap the concrete steps down to the lobby with its cracked front door window. Outside, dusk is falling. Streetlamps glow to life, throwing tiny shadows from buildings, parked cars, the forms of children playing ball in the street.

"So you have no possessions, right? You just travel?"

"More or less. I follow Spirit, intuition. I go where I'm needed, and sometimes just where I *want* to go. Like right now I'm just checking on Laura and Theodore. My friends."

"I'm a traveler, too. Kind of." We enter the store.

"I remember! A young time traveler!" He snatches up a basket from a stack by the cash register and begins to navigating wooden bins crammed with produce.

"Joe, with yoga and stuff—meditation and all that—do you think time travel is possible?"

"Hmm." Yogi Joe squints. "Travel to any place within the field of all possibilities is feasible. We can go anywhere, do anything."

He snatches an onion from a bin and holds it up.

"Consider…this is the universe." Yogi Joe traces the exterior with a fingertip. "At first glance, it's a simple sphere. But the exterior layer can be peeled back. Not everyone can see that. But if you can perceive it, I suppose, then that opens up possibilities."

He drops the onion into the basket with a smile then turns toward a barrel stocked with apples. Motion shimmers in the grocery store window. I see an edge. A corner. Then a gabled roof and—

Phil.

I hurry toward the door. The huge balloon man stands in a spill of light from a streetlamp.

"Hey, hi. How are you?"

"Fine, thanks." Phil is obviously packing up his wares for the night, gathering up string, deflating unbought balloons, tightening the wheel on his helium canister.

"Phil, what did you mean earlier? About not being where you belong, and about us being the same?"

"Haven't figured that out yet?"

I shake my head.

"Chris. I'm one of you. I'm Chronox."

My heart clutches up in my chest. I do not breathe for a whole minute.

"From what time period?" I ask.

"None. All. It's all the same, really. I'm one of many exiled to this time period. They like the Nineteen-Sixties."

"Who?"

"The Archon and his inner circle. They like this time period because it's a handy dead-end in which to exile your father's enemies. Oh yes, I know…"

"Who I am?"

"Yes. And I don't hold it against you. They think the Nineteen-Sixties is a time of negligible importance. But the cultural impact of the period? So many of the great artists and thinkers of this decade are exiles like myself—Chronox seeking to influence the trajectory of human development in the direction of love and peace. They lend this decade its richness."

"Maybe I'll stay here then. Be an artist—"

"No. Chris. You're the one person who can change it. The path the Archon has planned for this world. For you to be an artist would be a waste of that potential. Your talent is as a warrior, a philosopher, a game-changer. We're counting on you. Remember that."

Phil tips me a salute and wheels off down the sidewalk. I hurry back into the market.

"Yogi Joe, if you traveled back in time to where you were a day ago…would you see yourself?"

Joe freezes. And he turns to me, and the look on his face is like that of a man who has just seen a ghost.

~ * ~

It is Theodore who teaches me non-standard tunings. He demonstrates how to re-tune the guitar such that not only different chord voicings; but also entirely different complexions of sound become possible. I am really excited to learn this stuff. Theodore's alternate tunings open doors to musical places that up 'til now have been impossible to reach, same way Yogi Joe's meditation techniques show me parts of myself I didn't know existed. We are sitting in the living room passing the guitar back and forth when someone knocks on the door. Laura hurries through from the kitchen to answer it.

Tara stands there in a business suit, briefcase dangling from one hand. Checking the gold watch on her wrist. She has aged since the last time I saw her. Laura notices, too.

"Chris here?"

"Uh, yeah. Come on in…"

"No time." Tara checks her watch again. Pins me with her gaze. "C'mon, Chris. We need to go. Now."

Theodore's hands fall from the guitar. The room holds its breath as he gazes from Tara to me and back again. "But…Chris just got here," he mutters.

Tara ignores him. Without pausing to consider any alternative, I push upright and hurry to the door. Begin pulling on sneakers.

"Hasn't been any trouble, has he?" Tara sounds infinitely bored as she asks this.

"No," Laura answers firmly. "Chris is wonderful. In fact, we'd like it if he could stay longer."

"Not gonna' happen. C'mon, Chris!"

Theodore has risen to his knees with the guitar. Laura's jaw clenches and I am suddenly in her arms, surprised by how fast she moves and the strength of her grip.

"You take care, little brother, and get your ass back here real soon," she whispers fiercely. "Or I am gonna' be pi-iss-ed off at you! Understand?"

"Y…yeah." My throat hitches around a sob.

Laura releases me and steps back. "He can come back and visit, right?" she demands, tone suggesting Tara better consider the consequences of answering negatively.

Tara hesitates. The girl who hurled me into the past as a kid seems reluctant to displease the hippie chick who stands, arms crossed, staring her down in the doorway of a tenement in a long dead world.

"Sure. Now, come on Chris…"

She drags me into the hallway. The apartment next door is open. Beyond its threshold lies the kitchen of Uncle Leo's cottage. We step through. Tara closes the door. I take a seat.

Night presses against the windows.

"We don't have much time," Tara says, selecting a folder from the briefcase. "You're on a plane in two hours."

"To where?"

Tara has aged years as the timeline of her world continued forward while mine remained still. Her menace has deepened with adulthood.

"Back to the Facility. The Project has moved forward a considerable distance."

"Oh, yeah? How many more kids have you murdered?"

"Three and a half years have passed since I dropped you off with those hippies. Your father put you in time out to keep you out of the way. Well, time out's over. We've passed the first major obstacles. You can be released…conditionally. Your—"

"Three and a half years? You stole three and a half years of my life? What about high school?"

Tara's hand dips into her briefcase and comes out clutching a document that she slaps down onto the tray table. A high-school diploma in my name, dated that year.

"Any other questions, Chris? Want to see your health records for the past three years?"

Slap! A set of stapled medical reports covers the diploma.

"Your dental records?"

Slap!

"How about your fucking passport application?"

Slap! A stack of documents with a passport photo stapled to the top left-hand corner.

"Isn't it amazing what money can buy?"

I suddenly realize I haven't drawn a complete breath since Tara said the word "hippies." And that everyone my own age I've ever known—neighbors, classmates, even Tara and Dis—has moved on. I think of all the summer vacations, birthdays, Christmas holidays I missed out on. It isn't as if I ever had a lot of friends. But now the slightest possibility of ever connecting—of sharing anything—with them is lost forever.

"What about…junior prom? Graduation?"

"You missed out."

"Getting a…girlfriend?" My voice breaks.

"Chris, your time is past. Just get over it."

She checks her watch again.

"We've got a plane to catch. C'mon."

~ * ~

I stare out the oval of the Air Force passenger jet's window. The red light at the end of the wing burns eerily in the dark. Somewhere in the blackness beyond is Nevada.

The pilot's voice sounds over the intercom:

"Ladies and gentlemen, we're on final approach to our destination. Because we're entering restricted airspace, I'll have to ask that you stow all cameras and photographic equipment and switch off any recording devices. Also, please remain seated after landing until security personnel arrive to scan your passes and clearance paperwork. Thank you and have a pleasant stay at the Ranch."

I buckle my seatbelt as the Lear loses altitude. A sudden flicker of movement outside the window draws my attention. Canopy-glow and ID numbers are reflected in the taillight of an escort plane. An F-22 Raptor, wings bristling with weapons, has taken up station alongside us. A second one slips into place on the opposite side. They remain there for a full minute, inspecting the Lear before peeling off in a blast of noise to be swallowed up by the night. Two dotted lines of runway lights appear and then suddenly we are rushing along between them, the plane lowering itself on a cushion of gravity. After a bump, the whine of the turbines downshifts and we begin slowing. The pilot taxis toward the dark outline of what looks like a hangar. We stop and I hear the rumble of the hatch being unsealed from outside.

A man steps aboard wearing a black jumpsuit and gloves and holding a submachine gun. He inspects the cockpit, crew area and main cabin, then marches down the aisle toward the back, throwing me a subarctic glare as he passes. I hear him open the washroom door, inspecting the interior. Then the crackle of a radio and he speaks the single word, "Clear."

Home sweet home.

~ * ~

"Once you were gone, my involvement with the Project here at Nellis effectively ended." Major Gordon gestures toward the empty bookshelves, the bare table where we played chess, the wall with its faded patches where pictures once hung. "I was transferred. Cheyenne Mountain. In the years since we last spoke…"

Days, you mean, I think but say nothing, merely sit before his desk in a fresh change of clothes, handcuffed, staring back at him.

"…I've moved on to higher-level intelligence work. It's quite rewarding. I bought a house in Wyoming. Spend as much time there as we can…I got married…we have a daughter. By the way, did you know Tara has two chil—?"

Something in my eyes freezes the words in his mouth. It must be evident I'm not interested in Tara's welfare, nor do I care to hear about her wonderful, more or less chronologically intact life. I don't give a damn. About her. About anything. Except stopping Father.

"Listen, Chris, I'm sure you're upset. And I understand, let me tell you. But what your father is doing is important. Not that that makes things any easier, I'm sure. But resenting one's parents is normal for a boy your—"

"What did your father do, Major Gordon?"

"Ah…my father? My dad was a shoe salesman. Worked in a retail outlet in Spokane. When he found out I'd joined the Air Force, I remember he—"

"Did you have a best friend when you were my age?"

Major Gordon blinks. "Sure."

"What ever happened to him?"

"Charles? I think he's selling cars these days."

"I once had a friend. Wanna' know what happened to her?"

Something funny happens just then. Major Gordon's eyes play this weird trick in which they refuse to meet mine, lingering instead on the surface of his desk, as if believing that just by studying the dust there long enough, he can succeed in erasing my question. When he looks up, I pin him with a look that makes him squirm.

"You have no. Idea. What my life. Is. Like. So don't lecture me about boys resenting their dads. Okay, Major Gordon? It just sounds fucking stupid."

"Chris, I'm...I'm trying to be a friend—"

"I have no friends."

~ * ~

Intelligence is vital to the success of any military campaign and I have none. My first task must be to find out how far the Project has progressed. I begin by noting the changes in the Facility. There has obviously been a reduction in Facility personnel. The corridors, once packed with technicians and military personnel, now echo hollowly whenever I am escorted from the dorm to the clinic or Major Gordon's office or the storeroom for my daily beatings. There is also a new, glass-walled laboratory I walk by on my way to karate. I am careful to study its details each time I pass. Over a period of days, a complete picture emerges.

The machine they have been constructing seems to be finished. The short moving walkway, similar to the ones in airports, glows under a battery of high-powered lights and the army of white-coated technicians swarming over its every gleaming inch is bigger than ever. A sort of steel archway has been constructed at the far end. Periodically, some mechanism is activated that causes a field of shimmering blue light to crawl across the archway's aperture. Claxons sound each time the light appears, and the majority of technicians withdraw behind a set of blast doors. Then the light subsides, the claxon stops, and the technicians return to resume their minute inspection of the machine's chassis.

Another change I notice has to do with an alert. Last time I was here, alerts were sounded rarely. A tone would reverberate over the public address speakers, followed by a calm female voice intoning the word code and then a color. Now I hear them more frequently, but it's always the same: code orange.

A code orange is called one time as I am being escorted to

karate. The guard, a man I have never seen before, tells me to turn and face the wall until it's over. I do. A stampede of running feet fills the corridor behind me. I hear the clank of automatic weapons shifting in gloved hands, the labored breathing of men on the move as their combat boots pound the concrete. When it's gone, I am told to turn back around.

"Where's Fred?" I ask.

"Transferred," the guard replies.

"And what about those kids? The ones they were experimenting on?"

He says nothing.

CHAPTER EIGHT
Chess

I wait three months before making my first move.
I want Father to think he has won.

~ * ~

All great commanders demonstrate a willingness to learn from their mistakes. I am no great commander, but I do wish to emulate one. So in this I begin to assess my own defeats.

Twice I have escaped the Facility and twice been captured and returned. Why? These attempts failed because they were flights in space *only*. They took place in the physical reality of this When, where I am at a complete disadvantage. That sort of one-dimensional thinking is simple for Chronox to exploit. In order to have a chance, I have to escape the facility in time as well as space.

Given my limited Tipping ability, I can only go back or forward a day in time. Which means that to Tip to yesterday is only to Tip back into this same prison. So that's not a credible avenue.

As near as I can figure the scientists developed their Machine as an outgrowth of the Tipping Room at Uncle Leo's cottage, and then tested it on live Chronox subjects—mostly teens—until they perfected it to the point at which it was deemed safe for humans to use. I have no doubt Father intends to turn the technology against those sponsoring its development. His plans are grandiose enough that an agreement with the U.S. military can be considered, from his vantage, an annoying wrinkle to be ironed out at a later date.

In the meantime I resolve to continue meditating and conducting my experiments with Tipping on my own in an effort to improve my capabilities, so I won't be dependent on the machine as humans are. But I will also study the Machine.

~ * ~

Airman Ryerson's spinning back kick smashes my solar plexus. I slam into the wall shoulder-first and sink, dazed.

"C'mon, Chris! Get up!"

I shake the stars from my head and roll upright, taking a defensive stance, eyes narrowing in rage.

"Tha-a-t's it," she whispers with a smile. We circle. "Get angry! You a fighter? Or a momma's boy?"

"I'm a fighter, sensei."

"Then come get me."

Punch. Block. Sweep, kick. I dodge out of the way. She comes in a little deeper than is wise on her next kick and overbalances. I take advantage of the mistake to whip in and blast her ribs with a four-punch combo then slip back before she can retaliate. I can tell by her sharp inhale and measured retreat she is hurt.

"Good," she whispers.

"Thank you, sensei."

"But you're gonna' pay for that."

"Well then come on! Are you a fighter? Or a little fucking girl?"

A look of shocked anger ripples across her face before she comes at me with a snarl. I yell and launch myself into her attack. We meet halfway, no hesitation: all-out war.

This isn't me, I think, blocking a punch. *I'm not this guy. I'm not this vicious, angry warrior.*

But karate is making me one.

I don't think about anything—not my circumstances or my fear or how the black belt sensei Ryerson wears overshadows my white one. I just want to hurt her. For an eternal minute we are a furious halo of motion. Somewhere on my body, a blow lands that I barely register: my arms are machines that go right on hitting. Sensei's hands flash, distracting me before a white-hot pain explodes in my skull and I hit the floor.

"Chris? You okay?"

I shake my head to clear the fuzz.

Ryerson is beside me on her knees. "That was really good, Chris. You—"

Code Orange, Code Orange. All personnel assume D formation. Code Orange.

"Shit," she murmurs.

"What's up?"

"Lesson's over. C'mon."

Hoisting me upright, Airman Ryerson slings an arm around

my shoulder and moves me to the door. The claxon is sounding, alternating with the Code Orange announcement over the 1-MC. We pass the glass-walled laboratory where a blaze of light fills the room. I hold my hand up against the glare. Hatches slam shut, their indicator panels reddening to secure status all around us as we negotiate the stairs, then the final few meters to my quarters.

"Assume D formation means go to your assigned duty station. In your case, that's here."

Airman Ryerson keys a PIN code into the lock panel and the door slides open. I find a wall. Lean against it as she releases me.

"You really clobbered me at the end, there, sensei," I say as if reluctant to part (although what I really want is to keep an eye on the hallway).

"Back-fist. Tagged you on the temple. Any harder and I might have killed you."

A detachment of soldiers in field gear run by outside. In the split second I have to examine them, I note how each wears a round shoulder patch sporting a red hawk on a gold background. Then they are gone, obviously bound for the lab.

Interesting.

"You fought well today, Chris. I'm proud of you."

We face one another and bow. Then she steps out and closes the door behind her.

Locked in. Again.

It is late afternoon, so Major Gordon has gone home. There will be no interruptions for the next several hours. I enter my dorm, sink to the floor, and empty my mind.

Since my experience in the alley at the street fair, I am curious to see if meditation can further unlock my Tipping abilities. So another self-imposed step in my daily routine is to sit with back straight and shoulders relaxed, working my mantra until I feel that ticking at the far edge of my consciousness and a sensation of falling. It comes now more easily than ever, drawing me into the swirling Discontinuity...

From outside, voices:

...really clobbered me at the end, there, sensei.

Back-fist. Tagged you on the temple. Any...

The next words are drowned out by stamping boots as a detachment of soldiers in field gear sprint past. Then:

...well today, Chris. I'm proud of you.

A pause and I hear the door close behind her.

The first steps in a workable escape plan fall neatly into place. I smile before dissolving back into the present.

~ * ~

"...which is why they developed the base here in the first place." Major Gordon frowns down at the chess board. "The Facility is very remote. Real private. Allows us to try things out without interference from outsiders. New things like your family's project." He moves his bishop to attack my flank.

"I thought it was our company, TimeSygn, that's building the technology."

"Oh, it is! But sometimes, Chris, when new technologies emerge that have national security applications, the military partners with civilian experts to develop and deliver the product. That's why TimeSygn is headquartered here at the Ranch. Like Lockheed was when they built the U-2 back in the Fifties. Watch your rook, there, by the way."

"And the project itself? Its national security application is...?"

"Something I probably shouldn't discuss."

We play in silence for a few more minutes, before I ask, "Major?"

"Mm?"

"Question for you. I was wondering about Air Force Divisions and insignias. The one you wear is?"

"This?" He touches the winged globe encircling a key on his shoulder. "Stands for the Intelligence Division."

"There's one, too, that looks like a chessboard."

"Air Traffic Controller."

"How about a red hawk on a gold background?"

The moment the words leave my mouth I know I have struck a nerve. The Major starts as if receiving a sudden electrical shock. He is careful to avoid my gaze as he makes his next move.

"Sorry," he murmurs. "Can't help you." Then, gathering his wits, he looks me straight in the eye.

"There is no division or unit within the United States Air Force with that insignia. None at all."

~ * ~

The final piece of intelligence falls into place the next day.

Like any prisoner, I know my jailers' routines by heart. From the low humming of the floor polisher in the hallway each night at 10 PM to the sudden random activation of the desktop computer in Major Gordon's office that means the system is backing itself up, I am intimately familiar with the rhythms of life around the Facility. They are mostly benign: the sounds of everyday maintenance. The sort of thing I'd ordinarily ignore if not for the isolation imposed on me. My awareness of the smallest details is heightened. I become so attuned to each nuance that any variation in routine is immediately noticeable.

Mornings, for instance. A buzzer sounds when the alarm system in the hallway switches off. There usually follows the whir of a motorized cart bringing staff down to the lab. Then a prolonged silence. I am making my way to the bathroom when the clatter of unscheduled footfalls outside the annex door alerts me something's up. I step over to my dorm door and listen.

"...and because Dexter's gonna' kill me when he finds out. Thank God my transfer's already come through!"

"Where you headed?" asks a second voice, this one accompanied by the jingling scrape of what could only be a spoon in an empty coffee cup.

"Fort Detrick..."

To my amazement, the door to my room shifts inward just then. One of them is actually leaning against the door.

"...Bio-warfare division. Samuels' group."

"Good gig," replied Spoon-in-Cup appreciatively. "You jump a pay-grade?"

"Yeah. It's about time, too. You were going for the same slot, as I recall..."

"Yeah, but, listen—no hard feelings. The posting here is cherry. I'm grateful you put in a good word!"

"No prob. So. You're familiar with Grade B2-7 bio-hazard containment procedures?"

"Of course."

"Good. Because it's a whole different ball-game in there."

"You mean in the lab? With the...what's it called?"

"Jump Slide. They're calling it a Jump Slide. Once it's activated, ultra-sonic frequencies open some kind of Quantum gateway. It's weird, man! Real Buck Rogers stuff."

"Cool." Spoon-in-Cup's voice holds a measure of interest. "Like a dimensional-door thing?"

"We're not actually sure because we have to leave soon after it's activated. See, the techs hit the ON switch, we do our B2-7 sweep and then a Code Orange is called. Once that's announced, we have one minute—one minute exactly—to leave the lab. The aliens who helped us build this thing—the Chronox? —say if we're in the room when the Jump process begins, the resulting electrostatic charge will fry the organs inside our bodies. Only one of them can withstand the force because they're born to it. But that's neither here nor there—they're never around."

A tremor of eagerness—of excitement—grips me. I hug the door, rapt.

"So," Spoon-in-Cup prompts, "the process begins, we sweep, Code Orange. Then am-scray?"

"Yep. After that, once the charge has abated and the gateway is safe for human use, the Team arrives."

"What Team?"

"Phoenix/Gold."

A low whistle. "Whoa," Spoon-in-Cup whispers.

"Yeah."

"So. Jesus. They send a Phoenix/Gold Cell team? Why?" The spoon jingles again and his voice bubbles with nervous laughter: "Does something nasty jump in from another dimension when the Slide activates? Something dangerous enough to merit those killers?"

"I dunno." The door bumps again as Low-Voice moves off down the hall. "All I know is; we step away and the Team come in. And by the time we get back, they're gone."

"How long are we out of the room?"

"'Bout three minutes."

"Weird," Spoon-in-Cup says, his voice drifting down the hall. "So when we…"

The rest is indistinct. But that doesn't matter. I now have everything I need.

Whether the battleground is a field, city or chessboard, a great commander studies the terrain carefully.

I smile.

Our chessboard is time.

~ * ~

I sink to the floor and close my eyes.

The sense of falling begins almost at once. Confident now in my ability to navigate the past, I tumble into the Discontinuity. Moments rewind. I do not focus on any one in particular but try instead to simply experience them flipping backwards in sequence like playing cards. There is one very specific moment I seek and for which, dressed in my white karate gi and holding a square of cardboard, I have carefully prepared. To focus now would stop the flow.

Seconds gain speed, lengthening to become minutes. My disorientation deepens. I sense the events of the previous day buzzing around me like a cloud of bees as I sit amidst them, cross-legged and invisible. Doors close and open as Major Gordon comes and goes, along with previous versions of myself exiting and entering the dorm in a flurry of activity, doing everything backwards.

Minutes liquefy into hours. Evening, afternoon, morning, night, evening, afternoon...

Here it comes, I think. *Now slow it down.*

I grope for firmness within the Quantum quicksand. The hours slow to a crawl and harden into manageable quarter-hour chunks. These become brittle and fragment into minutes. I allow the flow of time to decelerate, pool into stillness and then shift direction from backwards to forwards. I hear shuffling nearby. Myself changing for karate the afternoon Airman Ryerson knocked me cold just before the Code Orange. I watch me put on an earlier version of the gi I now wear, wind the white belt around my middle and step out the door. Then I draw a deep breath and feel myself solidify into the moment. Stand. Take up the cardboard. Move to the dorm door and listen.

When I hear the clank of the entrance, I peer out in time to see my own white-suited back vanish into the corridor beyond in the company of the guard. Moving quickly, cardboard held before me like a weapon, I succeed in slipping it between the door and jamb the moment before the lock engages.

A breath. Two breaths.

No alarm.

Success!

Somewhere down the hall, an earlier version of myself is bow-ing to sensei Ryerson in the storeroom, preparing to fight for his life. Across the hall from there, techs in the glass-walled lab ready themselves for a Code Orange.

If we're in the room when the Jump process begins, the resulting electrostatic charge will fry the organs inside our bodies...

I wait.

...only one of them can withstand the force because they're born to it...

And wait.

...that's neither here nor there—they're never around.

I hold the cardboard in place, confident I can let go but unwilling to chance it. I have calculated too many variables, planned for too many unforeseen contingencies (like wearing the gi in case I am spotted) to risk all on such a small thing going wrong. I need that door accessible. So I stand pinching the edge of the cardboard, legs bent to ease my weight, breathing deeply, preparing. And remain that way for forty-five minutes.

Code Orange, Code Orange. All personnel assume D formation. Code Orange.

I crack the door and peer out.

The hallway is empty. I sprint for the stairs and take them two at a time down to the lab level.

Beyond the glass, personnel are scuttling from the room via a blast door in back. Before the final repetition of the announcement, the last one closes the door behind him.

Pinpoints of light flicker at the far end of the Jump Slide.

I cross the hallway. The mutter of Airman Ryerson's voice is now audible from the storeroom as she hoists the earlier version of me aloft, urging me toward the door...

The pinpoints of light have coalesced into a corona of brightness like a mouth opening in air, bright sparks of time-fire blasting into this reality from some other. The artificial Discontinuity. It pulsates, shifting and murmuring, its glare the brightness of a supernova.

I shoulder into the lab just as the lock on the store-room door clicks. Slowly, it swings open...

Holding a hand up to shield my eyes, I flee down the walkway toward the aperture's blaze. I have no idea where this time tunnel leads. But I close my eyes and sprint through.

CHAPTER NINE
Every Dark Tomorrow

Light claws my eyes. I shut them; arms extended to feel my way through the unutterable brilliance. The blood vessels in my eyelids glow scarlet, fade to gold, then white as the glare of Discontinuity cuts through the thin membranes to flood every last millimeter of my brain. I scream and raise my hands, the outlines of their bones clearly visible through flesh and clenched eyelids. I am still screaming when I tumble through the blaze and out into cold darkness.

~ * ~

I am on the floor of a ruined building. Shattered walls grope the sky, twisted ribs of girders visible where the concrete is shorn away. Chunks of it litter the ground now in jagged shapes, intermixed with triangular shards of glass that glimmer dully in rhythm to the explosions outside. Another one blossoms, its glare arriving instants before the shockwave lifts and hurls me onto a pile of dirt in one corner of the room.

A hand touches my shoulder.

I look up.

The eyes of the girl gazing down at me are the same color as her hair: ebony dark. Her face narrows from prominent cheekbones to a full, expressive mouth. She turns toward the next explosion, a strand of hair falling to cover one eye before she looks back and mouths the words:

Follow me.

I stumble to my feet. Toeing my way across ground carpeted with sharp edges, I note the explosions outside spacing themselves further and further apart until they fall completely silent. But a source of light continues glowing from somewhere. I look back.

The time-aperture still hangs sparking and twisting in the dusty air. The ebony-eyed girl catches me watching it. Then she turns and leads the way out of the ruins, light from the Quantum glare throwing exaggerated shadows onto the broken walls.

The landscape outside is a dark ocean of shattered buildings as far as the eye can see. The sky beyond is black, with a ribbon of molten red cutting the horizon while stringy clouds silhouette a moon the color of rotten oranges. An awful smell cloaks everything: a mixture of spoiled candy, spilled gasoline, and dog shit. The odor smacks me like a fist, plugging my nose and bringing tears to my eyes.

"It stinks here," I complain.

"It's the bodies." She speaks without turning. "The City's full of them."

I swallow, working to force the image from my mind.

"Where are we?"

She pauses and turns.

"We're in Hell," she says, then turns back to continue picking her way through the rubble.

~ * ~

We follow the remains of a street, its shape dimly visible among the shattered concrete and glass coating the City's remains. What hasn't been smashed to bits is vaporized. Something resembling a weird metal plant in bloom occupies the middle of one sidewalk. It takes me a second to recognize it as an iron streetlamp that has melted under the force of some volcanic heat. Similar sights populate the chaotic landscape: the twisted faces of ruined clocks with hands frozen at odd, impossible hours, the charred woodwork of fire-blackened doorways, frames of automobiles whose steel skin has melted to twisted wreckage.

I hear voices behind us in the ruins followed by the flickering shadows of moving men.

"They're here!" The girl presses my arm, urging me down a set of steps that drop below street level.

"Who's here?" I whisper. The cool smoothness of the concrete steps under my feet is a relief.

"The soldiers." She pauses near the bottom step and draws an old tin lantern from behind a weathered board. Lighting a match, she touches it to the wick. "They arrive through the light tunnel—same one you came from. They're here to kill us."

Glancing back at the top of the steps and the ruins beyond, I say, "You guys seem to be doing a pretty good job of that yourselves. I don't understand why anyone would come to a world like this. To hunt down the survivors of…of whatever the hell happened here? What did happen here? It looks like World War III or something?"

The girl is probably no older than fifteen or sixteen herself, and very lovely. I feel an impulse to reach out and touch her face, followed by guilt and an uncomfortable stirring in my belly because I am certain she can read my thoughts as I experience all these things. But rather than answer my question, she steps around me and begins negotiating the long flight of stairs toward the darkness below.

"People are calling it the Realignment. The carnage, the devastation. Calling it that is a polite way of saying it's a war without actually using the word. Millions dead and they're concerned about using the wrong word."

"What year is this?" I step around a puddle of reddish liquid and broken glass revealed in her lantern's light.

"It's Year Five of the Realignment. In your terms, that would be 2117. You came here from the early Twenty-First Century, didn't you."

It isn't a question.

I am about to ask her name when the lantern picks out a glimmer in the blackness: a pool of water at the base of the steps. Arriving there, I note curved walls and an arched roof. The floor, partially covered by a thin layer of moisture, runs twenty feet before dropping into a trench fifteen feet across.

"The old subway," the girl says. "People traveled underground before the Realignment. Millions once lived here."

"What was the name of this city?"

She shrugs.

"Well, then what's your—?"

"Kaya!"

I jump at the voice booming from nowhere. A globe of light emerges from below-ground in slow stages. Puzzled at first, I squint into the dark until recognizing it as a lantern being carried up a wooden ladder. The voice, like the light, has come from inside the trench.

"David!" The girl, Kaya, smiles and moves quickly to the head of the ladder. The man stepping onto the platform is a dark-eyed, handsome eighteen. They reach out and embrace each other hard, lanterns swinging, humming in satisfaction as their bodies crush together. I feel an immediate stab of jealousy and look away.

Down below, at the distant edge of David's lantern light, subway tracks glimmer silver.

Kaya and David move apart, holding one another's gaze for a long moment. Then David's eyes swivel toward me like cannons. He squares his shoulders.

"Found another survivor? Is he one of us?"

"Well, he's one of us," Kaya replies reluctantly, "but not a survivor. He came through the light tunnel just ahead of the soldiers."

David's expression hardens and he thrusts his lantern upward. In the widening circle of light, I can sense his personal power. He is a forceful man, perhaps something of a bully. I feel the need to assert myself right away by saying something. Anything.

"I don't understand why soldiers are coming here from the past," I offer. "It doesn't make any—"

But before I finish speaking, three things happen very fast.

The first is that David's face twists into an expression of cold fury. In the lantern light, he has seen and, apparently, recognized something he hates.

The second is that he steps forward and slaps me on the side of the head with such force my skull rings.

And finally he thrusts his face toward me and snarls, "They're coming here because you sent them! Think we don't know who you are? You're Chris Mitchell! It was your idea to send soldiers into the future to wipe out the remaining Chronox. Son-of-a-bitch! How dare you show your face here!"

~ * ~

"I say we kill him!"

David's face, ablaze with passion, draws rapt stares from the dozen-or-so refugees clustered around us on the ruined subway platform. It is here the last Chronox have made a home, safe from the Realignment's devastation and the Phoenix/Gold operators who blow in periodically from the past to hunt them. With their rags, matted hair, and bearded menfolk, they seem every inch the prehistoric tribe. And handsome, strong-voiced David with his energy and confidence is the obvious choice for leader—if he isn't already. They are drawn to him like magnetized needles to perfect North, drawing comfort from his presence.

The look of adoration on Kaya's face is most upsetting of all.

She loves David, is proud of him, and pleased to see him reaching new heights of prestige, even if (or perhaps because) it is at my expense.

"We have a unique chance, here! Before launching the Realignment, TimeSygn placed a timegate around this When so we couldn't Tip. We're stuck here, unable to fight back."

He pauses and rolls a hand in my direction as he adds:

"But then...this arrived."

I wish he would reach for me. Wish he would make a move, so I'd have an excuse to hit him. One good punch or kick and I could bring him down. But he landed the first unfair blow in our conflict and seems content to allow its memory to seep into my morale like acid. All he had to do is leave this status quo undisturbed to continue enjoying the upper hand.

"The history books tell us all about you. The little boy-tyrant who never grew up, who kept shifting around so he remained fourteen forever! But you drove yourself mad doing it."

"Fifteen," I say, hoping to trip him up. But it doesn't work. David is far too skilled at playing to the gallery to allow such a small contradiction to derail him.

"I can only assume he ended up here by mistake! He must have figured he'd gotten us all! Came to gloat, believing he'd achieved complete control over time travel on Earth. But instead of our dead bodies he's found us here alive and well, the war he'd started against us unsuccessful. The Corporation he founded may have absorbed the governments of the world...but it hasn't conquered us!"

These words vanish below a tidal wave of cheering. David has the Chronox in his pocket. He is their bright light in darkness and is burning fiercely. And there among them sits sweet-faced Kaya, applauding and grinning with admiration as David slices me to ribbons.

I close my eyes.

So history was rewritten. Instead of the victim, I was recast in Father's role: founder of TimeSygn and instigator of the Realignment. The final spade full of dirt on my life.

Wait.

It takes me a moment to recognize it. But once recognized, the truth cannot be ignored. It strikes me full force as I sit enduring the jeers and hateful looks of my own kind, prepared to offer my throat to David for the ritual blow.

Wherever Father is, whatever has become of his organization, I am here at the furthest frontiers of his empire, in the hands of those he hates more than anyone—the only ones who can threaten his control. I am at their mercy, yes. But effectively—and for the first Time—beyond Father's reach. It is as much of a fighting chance as I am ever likely to get.

But how to deal with David?

I rise.

"David's told you the truth!" I cry.

This gets everyone's attention. Especially his.

All warfare is based in deception.

"The truth, or—" I smile "—that piece of it that suits his purposes!"

I note expressions of interest passing between several of the elder Chronox men at this. A few smile, turning hard looks toward David as he stands isolated in the glare of my assault. I sense his popularity is not entirely universal.

"It's true I founded TimeSygn and did some pretty nasty things. But what David doesn't want you to know—"

"That's enough!" cries David.

"—what he doesn't want you to know—"

David opens his mouth to cut me off again but one of the men beats him to the punch, crying:

"Let him speak, David!"

David locks eyes with me. But remains silent.

I smile.

I have them.

"What David doesn't want you to know is that I've come back here to try and change things. I made mistakes. Sure. I know that! But the time has come for me to do what I can to fix them! David doesn't want you to know that because it might threaten his leadership. Because he senses not all of you are happy with it!"

I am careful to direct my next words to Kaya.

"Not all of you," I say quietly, eyes locking hers, "are happy with David's need to control everything."

It is more than his pride can bear. He shrieks and lunges at me, hands clawing for my throat. But I am ready for him.

My spinning back kick connects hard with David's solar plexus as he drives toward me, crashing the wind from his lungs and pitching him to the edge of the subway platform where he lands with a bone-smacking thud. I stalk toward him, cautious. He is moaning, hand to his chest, struggling to stand. I can tell he is partially shamming, hoping I'll grow overconfident and move in too quickly. But Airman Ryerson taught me well. As did Major Gordon. And Rommel. I stand just outside the range of his arm's reach, waiting.

Then he abandons the pretense and comes at me with a roar, trying to encircle my knees and bring me down. But I dodge away and slam a heel down firmly on his elbow, which shatters with a satisfying crunch.

Bastard, I think.

I circle in. Kick him hard on the face.

Vermin!

I drop to one knee and raise a fist to strike a final killing blow to his neck before stopping myself, dry-mouthed and trembling.

I rise and stumble away. A pair of Chronox women move forward to help him. I don't stop them.

I'm not about to let myself turn into Father.

~ * ~

The Corporation he founded absorbed the governments of the world...

Remembering these words, I flip through a magazine, its pages illumined by lantern-light in the little tent at the far end of the platform. A tent that had, until then, my guide assured me with a wink, been David's. The magazine's pages are tattered but still legible despite predating the Realignment. I don't recognize the title, *Currents*, but it proves a fascinating view of the world as it existed at the dawn of the Twenty-Second Century.

Automobiles ran on a form of non-polluting synthetic gasoline called dwahr. Schools were obsolete, except in the most backward Third World nations, with most English-speaking children participating in a universal form of computer-based home-schooling called Reach. Jazz music and Roman Catholicism were enjoying a cultural Renaissance, and the President of the United States was a retired heart surgeon named Ruus. The Toronto and New York stock exchanges had merged, and business was booming. And most every major corporation on Earth was partnered with—or a subsidiary of—TimeSygn.

Toyota/TimeSygn. McDonnell-Douglas-TimeSygn. MicroSygn Corporation. TimeSygn & ExSygn. And opposite page 36, a full-page ad:

TIMESYGN TIME TOURS
Consult Your Travel Agent!

One hundred and twenty years after its development, the Jump Slide's main purpose was tourism.

I flip ahead. Articles concerning the general election in Greater Brazil. A photo-essay about an architectural survey of Venice by submarine. Another on the newly renovated White House. There is one shot of President Ruus shaking hands in the Oval Office...

My breath catches in my chest.

...with Father.

"May I come in?"

Kaya stands at the tent flap. I set the magazine aside, fingers trembling. My initial attraction to her dampened as she applauded David's verbal mauling of me. But this sudden appearance makes me wonder what else of David's I might have acquired by giving him the beating of a lifetime.

"You busy?" she asks.

I say nothing.

She takes a step into the tent and crouches. "Look. I'm...sorry. About earlier, I mean."

"Which part of it? Your amusement at David's bashing me around? Or before that? When you met me and decided I was some new form of disease?"

"All of it. I was beastly toward you and I know it. I'm sorry."

Beastly. I smile. It is a quaint adjective; the sort you'd read in a British children's novel.

"May I stay?"

"Sure," I say with a sigh, scooting over to make room. I pick up the magazine. "I have some questions that perhaps you can answer."

"Of course!" She slides in beside me, thigh pressing mine. The ebony-dark eyes are on me, alive and insistent. I am puzzled by the sudden interest. Does she like me or just guys who win? I decide not to worry about it until later.

"Tell me anything you can remember about TimeSygn from before the Realignment."

Kaya's eyes follow my fingers as they flip back to the Time Tours ad and brush the corporate logo at the bottom of the page: a golden T orbited by stylized electrons.

"W...why would you ask about that? What can I tell you that you don't already know?"

"Look. I'm going to level with you. I'm not who you think I am. I mean...okay, I am. But not...*Rrrngh*! Jesus. How do I explain?"

Kaya observes my struggle passively.

"Okay." I close my eyes. "It's like this.

"I am my father's son. My father is the one who founded TimeSygn. He's the one who invented the Jump Slide and got the contract to develop it for the U.S. military. But he used me as the guinea pig to test it. See, I'm a Chronox who can't Tip...or I can, but only in very limited ways because I didn't start learning how until recently, and even then, had to figure out how all by myself. And not long after I did, he locked me away in this secret government facility and controlled my every move until I escaped here using the Jump Slide."

"Okay."

"I guess soldiers are coming here...what? On a regular basis?"

She nods. "You...I mean, your father...began hunting us back in the early Twenty-First Century. Things changed then. The way I learned it; there came a period of war and unrest and fear of terrorism. In response, governments became stricter...more laws, more police, more surveillance cameras. There was just more control over people in general and their activities. So it was easier to identify and track us down. A group of soldiers in the Air Force was founded called Phoenix/Gold whose area of expertise was 'Extreme Ops.' Things like assertive bio-hazard containment, recovery of stolen nukes, securing UFO crash sites, and...and hunting us. That's when CenterPoint was destroyed."

"CenterPoint." I remember the word being spoken by Tara a small eternity ago. "That was some kind of Chronox government council, right?"

Kaya is nodding. "The histories say it was created by the Chronox soon after their arrival on Earth, a place existing outside of time—where Chronox could go if they ever got lost or were in need of counsel. There was a man there named Anspach, the Keeper. He was killed when the Phoenix soldiers, the same ones who come through the light tunnel, invaded and destroyed the place."

I nod, the fog of confusion slowly lifting.

"The Chronox became increasingly isolated. Without Center-Point, we were stuck in our own little time periods and picked off one by one. Until the Realignment, when there were only a handful of us left. And now, it's only a matter of time." She laughs bitterly. "Time," she whispers.

We sit without speaking for the longest time.

"You didn't know any of this?" Her voice is husky.

I shake my head. "No more than I ever knew how to Tip."

"What was that like? Not being able to Tip?"

"Not being able to…? Kaya, I didn't even know it existed! I had no friends, no allies to show me. And the ones who could were too busy taking advantage of my inability to consider helping me. Like I said, I had to figure out how on my own. And even then, I can only Tip in one place. I haven't learned how to move through time and space simultaneously. Not that that would help me much now, given there's a timegate around this place."

She nods.

"Oh, and that's another thing I never learned—how to place timegates."

Kaya smiles. "My problem is the exact opposite. I know how to do all those things. In fact I'm told I'm actually gifted by Chronox standards. But it doesn't do me a lot of good here and now. For obvious reasons."

I gaze out the tent flap. From one end of the ruined subway platform to the other, lamps are going out in the make-shift tents and shelters of the refugee Chronox community. The profound stillness of the place—the weird sense of finality that comes from knowing it is impossible to Tip out of it—engulfs me. I remember my answer to Yogi Joe's question about what I'd do if I didn't have to go to school, how I said I would learn about myself. In the immense tranquility of a ruined world, it seems I will finally have the opportunity to do just that.

"Kaya?"

"Mm?"

"Tell me about timegates."

~ * ~

A weird mist clings to naked scaffolding and hills of shattered brick. Kaya glides effortlessly through the ruins ahead as I struggle to keep up, mind still reeling from all I've learned. In a single sleepless night of conversation, Kaya unveiled the mysteries crippling my life, affording me a glimpse of horizons I hadn't known existed. With the discovery came dizziness, and some anger. If I'd known more of this stuff early on, I could have lived a much fuller life. But of course Father needed a test subject for his Tipping Room. Gazing across the ruins of the TimeSygn-inspired Realignment in the full morning light, I have to wonder if it was worth it. *What difference does it make now?*

Kaya proposes, in the silence of the still-slumbering camp, that we climb back to the surface and take a walk. I agree, trusting she knows when it is safe to re-emerge from below. I follow her through the ruins of the shattered city. Kaya is my first Chronox friend.

"See there. That golden glow?" She pauses and puts her hand on my shoulder, pointing to the horizon. "That's the Consortium's edge."

"Consortium?"

"The area that's accepted Realignment. Once people submit to the new regime, the force shield is extended to cover their territory and the reclamation crews move in. People say they have these special robots that can rebuild an entire city in days."

"Why don't the people here do that?" I glance around at the sea of ruins. "Accept Realignment, I mean?"

Kaya leads us through the weirdly distorted rectangle of an iron doorway inexplicably left standing while the building to which it was attached became vaporized. "A lot of people have become accustomed to living like this—scavenging in the ruins for what they need. A lot of our people scavenge for forbidden items and so have their own reasons for wanting things to stay the way they are."

"Because…?"

"Under Consortium law, we're classified as terrorists."

"So why send the Phoenix/Gold soldiers from the past to hunt you, then?"

Kaya pauses beside a waist-high ruin inset with what appears to be fans or blowers of some kind. I recognize them as the kind of ventilator housings that sit atop freezers. The ruin around us is apparently the remains of a grocery store.

"This place," she says, "is useful."

"Isn't most of the food rotten by now?"

She moves toward a mound of concrete beams that have tumbled from the roof in more or less uniform sections. Tilted grey slabs tent upward at the jagged gap in the roof. Kaya places a hand on one slab, lowering a leg down through the triangular opening then pausing. "The food's spoiled," she admits, "but there's other stuff: utensils, containers, things like that. Condiments and seasonings that don't expire for a period of years—if you can find any unbroken containers. Also junk that customers left behind when the shelling started."

I gaze dubiously into the wreckage.

"Come on," she urges.

I follow.

Ducking below the apex of the makeshift tent, I am engulfed again in that spoiled-sweet mix of decomposition. Kaya must have noticed my discomfort because she fishes in her pocket and comes up with a set of swimmer's nose plugs. "Here, use these. I salvaged 'em from the old pharmacy for myself. Don't need 'em anymore."

"You're used to this?"

"Yeah."

I adjust the nose plugs until they're comfy, then look around. A spill of stones and earth slope downward from the triangular aperture through which we'd climbed, broadening into the floor of a huge subterranean space. Poking up through waves of dirt illumined by the dull gray light from the gaps above are snouts of shopping carts, jumbled mounds of broken products, fragments of walls, doorways, and sharp corners of shelving. Kaya picks her way through this toward a shallow trench.

"I've been digging here, excavating for—"

A shaft of golden light sails through the cavern diagonally toward us. No sooner do I notice it than Kaya is grasping two handfuls of my gi and dragging me to the ground, covering my body with her own.

"Don't move," she whispers, lips moist against my ear.

A burst of radio static fills the air. Then a voice mutters, "Tango, two-six. Clear."

I hold my breath and close my eyes, reaching out for the slightest scrap of intelligence with my ears, skin, intuition. Phoenix /

Gold has arrived.

I hear a crunch of gravel, another burst of static. The voice creeps into my awareness again, this time from farther away. "Some kind of cave…artificial," it says.

There's a pause before another voice responds, "Roger."

A footstep and a crumble of rocks sliding in from the triangular aperture of the entrance. I hear the scrape of something metallic (a gun? a helmet?) against saw-toothed concrete and then a final short burst of static before silence returns.

"Listen," Kaya hisses, "we're going to Tip."

I turn my heard to reply. Her palm forces it back into place on the earth.

"I know you think you can't, but you can. You must. We're trapped here. So listen…"

A crunch of footsteps, then the clank of equipment as the soldier moves down into the cave. I hear his sigh echo through the artificial caverns of the collapsed roof.

"…enter your meditative trance. When I squeeze your arm, I want you to think the word, *seye'la*."

Footsteps crunch gravel at the far end of the cave. Softly.

"If we don't Tip," Kaya says with a hiss, "we'll die."

Despite the uncomfortable weight on my back and the sharp rocks pinching my chest, I close my eyes and begin the sequence as best I can. Spine straight, shoulders relaxed…tongue…

Another stirring of rock. A flicker beyond closed eyelids that senses the light beam moving over wreckage.

Tongue relaxed on the floor of my mouth. Slowly, the disorientation swims in and I surrender to it. The ticking begins at the edges of my…

"Hey!"

The definite sound of footsteps. One. Two.

"*Stand up!*"

I plunge into the dizziness behind my eyelids, fear tugging at my belly, and think the word *seye'la*. Nothing happens. I hear the snap of something being released and a spray of machine-gun fire that mutes, softens, turns itself inside out until it is only a dull echo, then an auditory negative of itself.

I open my eyes.

We are face down at the top of the steps to the subway

platform.

~ * ~

Meals at the Chronox camp are a communal affair. Although there is no set time for eating, we manage to congregate more or less simultaneously, drawn by some tribal instinct to the open space on the subway platform where David and I fought. A large iron pot is produced from a storage closet once used to house janitorial supplies and set in place over an odd blue ring enclosed in steel mesh. Kaya explains it is a dwahr stove from before the Realignment. Someone named Margaret found it in the ruins of a camping supply store.

Margaret turns out to be one of the two Chronox women who helped David after I was done with him. She eyes me skeptically as I move forward in line to receive my bowl of stew the night of my and Kaya's encounter with the soldier in the ruins.

"Nice day?" Margaret asks primly.

I nod.

"David's gunnin' for you," she says, peering down her nose at me.

"He had his chance," I snarl, pushing my bowl forward.

She hesitates a moment before ladling out a serving. Then, collecting herself by wiping her hands on a dishtowel, she changes tack. "I wouldn't be feeling so high and mighty if I was you," she cautions.

"Oh, yeah? Why's that?"

"David's loved here. He has friends."

"So do most dogs."

"Oh, you're a tough one, ain't ya'? Think yer all that, don't'ch'ya? Prob'ly had all the world to yourself for years, eh?"

"Christ, don't you have any salt to go with this?"

"Beware. You're as good as dead!"

"Ain't we all?" I sigh and move away.

The Chronox mumble and scuffle around the edges of their encampment on the platform, tumbling onto benches and cushions as they negotiate the chaos that is their home. I examine them, feeling a surge of pity for the group. I have yet to meet many of them but feel a bond of kinship that blurs to outrage when I consider all we are capable of balanced against the state to which we are reduced. I search the edges of this assemblage for Kaya. She is seated on the edge of a wooden crate a few paces from the door of what I now imagine as our tent.

"Mind if I sit down?" I ask, shuffling in and lowering myself onto the arm of a ruined sofa beside her.

She smiles. "Are you alright?"

"I guess so. I—"

"CHRIS!"

I look up.

David. Crushed elbow bundled to his chest, he stands at the far edge of the platform, the Chronox scattering to clear a corridor between us as he screams at me, face sickly yellow, still bruised from where I'd kneed him. He hoists a pistol with his good arm.

"CHRIS! You bastard!"

I stand.

Kaya screams, "No!"

"CHRIS!"

I am ready for him.

Ready, the Hagakure and the ghost of Airman Ryerson standing behind me, prepared to take a bullet—two, even—if it means I can advance and get a hand on his throat before I die. I am even taking a step in his direction when the air reverberates with sudden boot-steps and I see a golden light-beam bisect the platform's darkness.

"CHRIS!"

"There! There he is!"

A scatter of voices swells the tunnel around us.

"CHRIS!"

Chaos, the station reverberating with sounds of submachine-gun fire, the screams and the specter of David, the back of his head disintegrating and Chronox scattering in a hail of bullets as the Phoenix/Gold team storms the station and takes control, knocking me unconsciou—

CHAPTER TEN
Incense and Handcuffs

"The CCTV image cut out just as you entered the Discontinuity." Major Gordon offers an apologetic smile. I say nothing, merely stare down at my cuffed wrists, doing my best not to remember the image of Kaya being blown to bits by machine-gun fire.

"When I arrived next morning, one of the security officers was waiting. Sitting right where you are now, in fact."

The Major's chuckle and head shake invite me to savor the irony, to believe he shares my distaste for the whole matter. I force myself to breathe, remaining perfectly still as his smile broadens, reaching its apex, then fading when he sees it is getting him nowhere.

He clears his throat and taps the edge of the desk with a pencil.

"They grilled me for hours," he continues briskly. "It's rather confusing but—near as I can make out—your disappearance left some loose ends. You somehow managed to Jump twice—once back to the previous major Slide activation and, from there, into…the future, was it? Is that right?"

He is fishing for information. Whether on his own behalf or Father's made no difference. I'm not planning to share. I take comfort in the knowledge Father hasn't yet figured out I can Tip on my own.

Silence.

His eyes flit away, searching the corners of the room with extravagant calm. He is frightened. This much is obvious, as is the fact he's been forced into a discussion he'd rather not be having. He has changed since we last spoke.

I live in a world of self-evident facts I alone can perceive.

Growing more frustrated, Major Gordon tries another approach.

"The entire Facility was in an uproar. They initiated a Code Omega search. Know what that means? Every single door in the place has to be opened. Can you imagine? Insane! Scent tracking dogs. Last-minute sector evacuations. Guys charging around with guns. Madness! No one was allowed to leave for two weeks. I slept here in my office."

I stare up and meet his gaze. Hold it for a long moment.

"You slept," I say, "in your office?"

He nods.

"How terrible for you. How, awful. Really."

"Chris—"

"No. No, really. My God, Major Gordon. Of all the *terrible* things to be endured. Hunger. Disease. War. Terrorism. Tyrannies and dictators inflicting torture on helpless civilians. Children born with radiation deformities and sick, pointless, unending cruelty and misery. And you! You, had to sleep in your office."

For the first time since meeting me Major Gordon seems on the brink of getting angry with me. His jaw firms. He sighs deeply. Then, swallowing, he manages to calm himself enough to speak. "Chris—"

"I'm going to destroy this place. If it's the last thing I do."

~ * ~

Something hardens inside me as I am marched through the corridors of the subterranean complex behind Tara. The thing hardening inside me is very much like a bullet, hard and shiny, point upward. My insides clench around it like the tight chamber of a gun. Ready to fire. I suppose it is a natural reaction. Everything that is rightfully mine has been stripped away: my origins, my identity, my friends—even my time has been stolen from me. I have nothing left except one secret: my ability to Tip.

I watch Tara and the guard brush past a technician pushing a cart, forcing him to stop and wait. She moves like a queen through the scientists, military personnel, and minor functionaries, all of whom are quick to scuttle out of her way. She is the elite. Untouchable. What initiation do you have to pass, I wonder, to be admitted to that inner circle?

I'll never know.

"You're being put in time out again," she informs me, "because, as you can see, we're busy right now. Lots to do, lots to do."

"Places to go? People to kill?"

"It's sad, Chris. You just never figured it out. Did you?"

"Figure what out?"

"How to be a...person. Whatever it takes to get ahead, to succeed. How to use situations and people to your advantage. How to grow up."

We arrive at the lab door. A trio of scientists glances up from their computer consoles as we enter. Two even stand briefly upon recognizing Tara. I am duly impressed. This courtesy complete, they return to their seats and continued fiddling with the controls.

At the far end of the slideway, points of light are flickering into existence as the Discontinuity emerges. I step through the doorway and hold my hands out. The guard removes the cuffs. I step to the entrance of the walkway, rubbing my wrists. Stop.

"Hey, Tara!"

Already halfway out the door, she turns back.

"What's going to come through that door five minutes from now?"

It takes her a second to recall the old childhood game she and Dis used to play with me. Once she does, she frowns.

"Not funny, Chris."

"Maybe not," I admit. "But my next joke will be."

"Oh, yeah? Does it have a good punch-line?"

I smile.

"Oh, you bet. Just brace yourself, Tara. Because you have *no idea* what's coming next."

I turn and walk into the flash and blast of the swirling time storm.

~ * ~

The bare bulb glowing overhead throws sharp shadows on the concrete walls. I step around a scatter of trash to the apartment door and knock. Laura's face upon answering shifts from caution through confusion to joy in a heartbeat.

"Hey!" She skips out and crushes me to her granny dress in a massive hug. I gasp and hug back, inhaling the smell of her: incense and girl-sweat and baking flour. A whiff of pot smoke drifts out. I can hear voices inside: Theodore's and Yogi Joe's. Sitar music hisses from the cheap speakers of the turn table.

"Lemme look at you." Laura thrusts me out at arm's length. "Gosh, Chris. You look…"

"How do I look?"

"I dunno'. Stronger. Is that possible? It's only been a month or so."

A month, I think. *Okay.*

She squeezes my biceps. "You been doing push-ups?"

"A lot of 'em," I answer. "I'm learning karate."

Laura frowns at the word "karate," plainly disapproving, but saying nothing aloud. She drags me down the narrow passage to the living room where a trio sits around the low table in smoky lamplight.

"Look who's here!" she cries.

Theo glances up. His beard cracks, unleashing a wide grin. "Chris! Hey, man!"

Yogi Joe springs up and enfolds me in a hug.

"Where's Sunshine?" I ask, unashamedly glad to see them all.

"In bed early. Can you believe it? She's been up 'til dawn the past two nights working on her great big mural project. Man, it's great to see you!" Theo claps me on the back, gesturing to the third man at the table. "Chris, this is Jake."

Jake wears an army fatigue jacket, headband, and sunglasses. He nods to me distantly from behind his smoldering joint.

"Jake's been telling us about Vietnam," Laura offers.

Something in Laura's voice makes me turn and examine her after she speaks. Quivering beneath the word "Vietnam" is the sort of tremor I experience when speaking to Father. *"He who fears his enemy is already defeated"*; I remember reading that somewhere. So Laura fears Jake. Confident, strong, self-assured Laura. This makes me wary.

Jake seems to be waiting for me to say something, so I oblige him.

"You in the military?"

Jake snorts as if I just asked a stupid question. Which, given the political situation in Southeast Asia in 1969, I probably have. Nobody goes to Vietnam as a tourist these days.

"Yeah," he says behind a brittle chuckle, "I was in the military."

"Which branch?" I snap, sensing a challenge.

"U.S. Army," he shoots back. "Fifth Infantry Division, Iron Triangle. I mustered out after Operation Cedar Falls."

"General Westmoreland going after enemy bases," I say quietly. "Mostly underground, as I recall."

Jake considers this quietly.

"Followed it in the papers, did ya'?" he asks. His voice is level, without any trace of emotion. No sarcasm. It appears I am touching on a subject he cares about.

"No. I studied the strategy involved."

Theodore and Yogi Joe exchange glances and I sense something shift around the table. A shared interest in strategy forms a bond between me and Jake that is not shared by the others.

"Wasn't much strategy to it, if you wanna' know the truth," Jake offers. He sucks on his joint and offers it to Laura (who refuses) and Theo (who takes a polite, shallow toke before handing it back). "After the bombers reduced the jungle to mush, we arrived. We knew the Cong were dug in, had some sense of the tunnel system but no idea how freakin' big it was! Me and the rest of the rats were sent—"

"Rats?"

"Tunnel rats." Jake toys with his joint as his eyes take on a far-away look. "Weren't much damned strategy to that, neither if you wanna' know the truth. Just a group o' smaller guys, like yours truly, armed with flashlights and Colt .45s. We went in and down. Echo Black. Total pitch night, man. Inching along step by step, never knowing if we were about to stumble onto a sentry or into a pit of sharpened bamboo stakes or nest of poison centipedes."

Jake snorts again, tapping the ash from his joint and fixing me with a beady eye.

"How old're you?"

"Fifteen." I ignore Laura's frown and sudden troubled stare.

"You thinkin' of joining up?"

"No."

"Good. Don't. You seem like a sharp kid. Tough guy. You'd do well in the Forces. But don't go. Into any army—even ours. Not while we're fighting that rat's nest over in 'Nam. Because a guerilla war is unwinnable. Even by the most powerful force on Earth."

I smile.

~ * ~

"Chris? Can I speak with you?"

Laura's formality and the way she hovers in the bedroom doorway tell me something serious is in the offing. Jake left a few minutes ago and I came in here to Sunshine's room at Theo's suggestion. The little girl is sleeping in Laura's bed to escape the paint fumes from her drying mural. Now hours later, with a window open, the smell from the chaotic tangle of color on the wall is bearable. I have already pulled off my shirt and socks and am making ready to hit the sack hard when Laura knocks.

She comes in and sits down on the bed.

"Chris. There's something strange going on in your life that has to do with time. Isn't there?"

I freeze. "Ah, look...I don't know what you—"

"Chris."

A frown tugs the corners of her mouth and she squares her shoulders. Her eyes bore into mine.

"I'm not stupid. Okay? So don't treat me as if I am. There's something going on with you. I can tell! That day at the street fair? When I saw you materialize in the alley by the newspaper machine? And the way your cousin Tara seemed to age by a factor of years in the two days between the time she dropped you off and came back to pick you up? And now you say you're fifteen? I'm sure you are. But the way you speak, and think are like someone very much older. And your eyes, Chris."

Her lips press together.

"Your eyes hold the pain of a much, much older person."

She pauses calmly for a moment before concluding.

"Chris. We love you. But if you're going to crash here you need to be honest with us. We have a child in our home. So cut the crap. And tell me what the hell is going on."

I stand frozen in shock. Poised midway between tears of frustration and a guffaw of relief, I teeter on the brink of another evasion. But gazing into Laura's earth-brown eyes and experiencing the love I feel for all of them as it swells within me like a tide, I can no more lie to her than I can stop breathing. She loves me. She loves her family. And will fight to the last breath in her body to protect both. In this, she is as heroic as any of the great commanders I have studied. *No soldier fights alone.*

"Laura?"

"Mm?"

I smile shyly. "There's something I haven't told you about myself..."

~ * ~

In the wee hours of the morning I am awakened by the

kree...kree...kree of Phil's balloon wagon. I roll to a sitting position by the window where the stirrings of dawn are softening the black square of night outside to darkest blue. I take a deep breath, close my eyes, and press my fingers to my closed eyelids.

OK, I'm here. With Laura, Theodore, and Sunshine. Not in the Facility anymore. It's...nineteen-sixty-something.

I see the balloon wagon appear and, behind it, Phil's huge bulk. He pushes his contraption off the curb as if intending to pass us by. But ten steps into the intersection he pauses and raises his head as if smelling something on the wind. Then he turns down our street and begins navigating his pushcart in the direction of our tenement.

Day comes on slowly as Phil draws level with our building and pauses. He pulls a fistful of balloons from his trousers and slowly he begins filling them one by one and tying them to the push bar. The big man works swiftly and quietly, the minute hiss of the helium canister audible in the quiet. The clutch of balloons grows steadily until they are a multi-colored flock of bubbles, green, blue, white, red. He fills one last one: black. Loops a string around it. Adds it to the clutch tied to the rail.

Suddenly, he begins unfastening balloons. Releasing each with a quick flick of his wrist.

As I watch them clear the rooftops and recede into the brightening sky, the big man takes up his cart and resumes his trek toward the far intersection. When I look down again, he is gone.

~ * ~

I snooze and wake again later. Clouds have rolled in over the city since Phil's balloon release. I hold my breath before opening the door.

Whispers entice me down the hallway toward the living room where Laura, Theo, Sunshine and Yogi Joe sit around the low table, talking. They pause and stare when I walk in. I stare back, sensing the chasm widening between us.

So it goes, I think. Another chance for connection lost. A herd of brightly colored bubbles rising into the sky without me. I stand on the ground, watching them go. Again. And again. And again and...

I feel like killing myself.

But I feel like killing Father more.

"Good morning, everyone," I say, the steel in my voice the result of the fact...I've just stopped caring.

Everything dies, I remind myself. *Everything.*

Theo is the first to speak. He glances to Laura, then Joe. But not to me.

"It's not that I think he's lying," Theo says gently. "But...ungh! Look...it's obvious Chris has been through a lot. Sometimes people, you know...experience things differently and see things a certain way because they've—"

Laura interrupts. "You think he's nuts."

Theo's eyes widen. "No! I don't thi—"

"Theo, if Chris is nuts then I'm nuts, too." The slant of Laura's eyebrows telegraph anger.

"Laura, we've both done our share of psychedelics. Maybe what you saw was an acid flashback. C'mon...admit it's at least possible."

Laura inhales sharply then sits contemplating the line of smoke rising from the incense burning on the table before them. From the hunch of her shoulders, I can tell she was ready to argue but is now prepared to concede Theo's point. Watching her in that instant, I know—even she can be made to doubt the evidence of her own eyes. I suppose anyone can. But I know Laura's doubt will throw my honesty into question and cause our friendship irreparable damage.

Everything dies, I remind myself. *Everything.*

Now that I know how to Tip in space as well as time, there is no need to remain here any longer. I turn and head for the door.

"Yogi Joe, what do you think?"

"I think Chris is telling the truth."

I stop.

"Chris. Please come in here and sit down with us. I refuse to speak about you in the third person while you're still in the apartment. And I'd like you to hear what I have to say. It may interest you. Please?"

It's hard, when you've allowed yourself to love people, to find them suddenly doubting you. I am so tired as I turn and walk the few steps back to the living room. Exhausted in a way I have never been before. I need so badly to be accepted, but instead find myself reliving: Peter, Lu, Kaya. All the relationships I've had. And lost. So I come within ten feet of the group and kneel down in *seiza* position, the one Airman Ryerson taught me for karate meditation.

I will not allow myself to love these people.

Everyone I love dies.

~ * ~

Yogi Joe breathes, calmly sorting through his thoughts. He seems uncharacteristically troubled as he begins.

"I haven't told anybody this. But last summer in Varanasi, I visited my guru. We were staying in an apartment by the river loaned to us by a friend. There were five of us, all long-time students of Gavananda-ji, and I guess it was what you could call an advanced seminar. The guru was lecturing on the path of the Sadhu."

Yogi Joe smiles.

"For those of us who wander, such times together are...very special. A small community develops within the ashram for the days or weeks during which we study, and ideas are shared. Common concerns emerge, guided by the guru, guided by Spirit. For some reason, this particular gathering found us all contemplating Kali."

"What's Kali?" Sunshine asks. She has been so still, so attentive, up until now, we forgot she was even present. But once she speaks up, we realize she is hanging on Yogi Joe's every word.

"Kali is a goddess, Sunshine. She's very powerful. And frightening. She has black skin, many arms and she dances so powerfully she shakes the world to its foundations. She is a destructive force."

"Is she a demon?" Sunshine asks.

"That's...actually a very difficult question to answer. I don't know. I'm not sure anybody does. But Gavananda, my teacher, believes that while Kali is associated with death and destruction, she is not Death itself. Rather, she is the goddess of Time and Change. She causes movement. Change. Motion from stillness. Life from death."

Sunshine considers this very carefully.

"That's very interesting," she finally says.

Laura and Theo exchange looks of surprise.

Yogi Joe nods. "Yes. I think so, too." He takes up the thread of his tale. "One night there was a terrible storm. Thunder and lightning exploded across the sky. One moment, it was calm; the next, the

Ganges was whipping against its banks. Trees and buildings shook. Everyone ran indoors, and even Gavananda and we students were interrupted in our meditations. We came out to the front room to look through the windows at the terrible violence outside. The power went out. Gavananda told us to close the shutters and light candles. He wanted to speak to us. So we did as he asked, lighting candles, and gathering together as the storm built outside.

"Gavananda said the spirit of Kali was powerful on the Earth at present. He said people often confused this period with the Kali Durga, an apocalyptic, that means 'end of the world', Sunshine, period associated with a demon who was also named Kali. But Gavananda said this wasn't the case now. That this was just a time of radical change. In fact, the very spirit of Time itself was becoming incarnate on the Earth. Gavananda-ji claimed there were time-dwelling creatures mentioned in the sacred texts and observed thousands of years ago by the ancient Hindus. These creatures came from another world. Gavananda said they would gain power over the societies of men, and their activities would lead to massive alterations in the nature of our world.

"Then he asked us to close our eyes.

"The guru led us in a powerful meditation. It seemed to go on and on. And when he asked us to open our eyes, it was daylight. But a weird kind of daylight—hazy and gray, cold and filled with something.

"We opened the shutters. What we saw horrified us. Instead of the city, just ruins as far as the eye could see. The river was choked with dead bodies. Dark smoke hung over everything. The sky was black, with a strip of dark red low against the horizon. And distant explosions shook the ground. Death was everywhere.

"Gavananda said what we were seeing was the result of a great war. Not the final war that would destroy everything, but a devastating conflict that would be caused by those time-dwellers observed by the ancients. Our guru said this war existed in the Absolute or, 'quantum field of all possibilities' not as a fact but rather a potentiality. It might or might not come to pass, depending on the actions of those responsible.

"Gavananda said that, while the time-dwellers were evil beings, like all spirits they had the free will to choose good or evil. He said it was impossible that not even a single one of them would choose to pursue personal growth over personal gain and work to frustrate the plans of his leaders. Gavananda said because he had faith at least one of them would choose good over evil, the things we were seeing very well might not come to pass. That there was still a chance to change the course the time-dwellers had charted for our world. And I agree with him."

Yogi Joe fixes me with an iron stare.

"Because you have a plan. Don't you Chris?"

CHAPTER ELEVEN
Titan

The high ground. In military terms, it's everything. In a two-dimensional land-based war, the ability to take and control a commanding height confers an advantage over the enemy. Because whether the campaign is being waged on horseback or hovercraft, nobody likes attacking uphill. Defenders enjoy a better view and the momentum conferred by attacking downward. If I was fighting Father in a land-based war I would seek high ground. But time is our chessboard; a battleground shaped and modified by the actions of the opponent. Three-dimensional, so the preference for the high ground does not apply. In this particular kind of war, the low ground is preferable.

Father controls the present, which means he controls the future.

So I have to control the past.

I step into Sunshine's room and close the door behind me. The window is open, and I shut that too. Fumes skirl like swamp gas in the closed area. I pick my way through paint cans to find a bare patch on the floor. I sink down cross-legged and watch shafts of light crawl through the cans, remembering that long-ago afternoon in Father's workshop when he slowed time so I would miss my chance to go to Peter's cottage with my friends. I remember the dust motes dancing in shafts of light, the weird sensation of time slowing and the Theremin sound wavering in my ears. And I remember being helpless.

I have learned to Tip. My own experiments, plus Yogi Joe's input and Kaya's tutoring have filled in all the missing pieces of the puzzle. I know I can do it, and what is more, I know because I was held back, restrained, for so long, I have developed the Chronox equivalent of muscle mass by dynamic tension. The ability to Tip better and farther than I otherwise would.

I straighten my spine, close my eyes, and begin breathing deeply and evenly. I edge toward the Discontinuity.

Time is our chessboard. All warfare is based in deception. And there is a story of an old Greek god called a Titan who was so fearful his offspring would grow to become more powerful than him that he chose to eat them as they were being born.

His name was Chronos.

~ * ~

I realize the first thing I need to do is to get my hands on a few things, including the laptop. Because no matter what happens, a record of all this must survive. So my first Tip is back to the Facility the afternoon of my second escape attempt, when I used the Jump Slide.

Seye'la, I think, descending into the formless void of the Discontinuity. The moments slow, crystallizing into discreet and tangible blocks of time. I sort through them carefully, looking for the precise moment when I rise from meditation, the strip of cardboard in my hand, and stuff it between the tongue of the lock and the jamb. I wait, hovering in the void, until the earlier me opens the door and bolts. Then I materialize into the dorm.

The laptop is on my desk. I grab it and stuff it into my backpack. And I think to myself—three. There are three of us. Three separate versions of Chris inhabiting this moment of the time/space continuum. My heads swims with the paradox. I take a moment and steady myself on the edge of the desk. Good thing they don't give tickets for breaking the laws of physics.

I consider my next steps.

I have to discover the tipping point at which Father gained the upper hand in his war against humanity. I will have to review his life from the beginning, slowly and carefully until I find the moment at which he gained decisive advantage. Then—

The PIN pad at my door chirps. Someone is coming in! I grab the backpack and dive into the kneehole of my desk. Pull the chair in. Hold my breath. Wait.

The door hisses open. Footsteps. As I look, the spit-shined toes of leather shoes appear. Major Gordon's. He is muttering to himself.

"...can't remember where I left them. Was it...?"

He rummages on the desk, his knees a foot away from my nose. I close my eyes. Draw a deep breath. Settle into my meditation routine and await the faint ticking at the edge of my consciousness.

As I feel my awareness teeter, I say the mantra Kaya taught me again and dissolve into the Discontinuity. The office, the desk, Major Gordon, and all vanish abruptly.

~ * ~

A thin rain is falling as I materialize in the distant past.

I've always wanted to learn more about the ancient world. The different eras and ages, the transitions Man made from tools of stone to those of bronze and iron, the building of pyramids and palaces. But I am on a tight schedule. So, instead of being enchanted by the plumed head-dresses of ancient Aztecs, I am shivering in a rainy wind on a vast plain in central India 6,000 years before Christ.

Through clouds, I see the huge shadow of our planet approaching Earth and remember Kaya's words about the origin of our people.

...another world. A world very similar to our own. Once every ten thousand years or so, the two planets pass close enough to one another to allow for transit.

The sphere of the looming body crams the heavens, its giant curve swallowing half the sky. Chronox, vaster than I've ever seen the sun or moon.

A great light blossoms in the atmosphere, followed by a sparking trail as a flame-jet descends through rain clouds.

The refugee ship.

No larger than a compact automobile and devoid of protrusions, windows, or markings of any kind, it is vaguely egg-shaped, the circular opening from which the exhaust flame sprouts being its sole exterior feature. The craft slows, rotating on approach. I duck behind an outcropping of rock. The flame cuts out twenty feet from the ground and the craft glides down to land among the grassy hillocks with a soft bump.

A hairline fracture appears, encircling the tip. It opens, releasing a blue-gold glow. Thin streams of smoke creep from the aperture to surround the ship in coiling tendrils, expanding and coalescing into a dense cloud of blue fog.

Static bursts within the blue haze. I see shapes drifting inside, an arm, a knee, a face in profile. A woman suddenly steps out into the misty rain and runs her hands down her naked body before holding them up before her face, eyes filling with wonder. Arms extended, she twirls about in the rain, face to the sky, the grunting ancestor of a laugh escaping her throat.

Others join her in the clear air beyond the blue cloud, Chronox morphing from energy beings into creatures of matter. The change occurs slowly and is obviously quite painful to some of them. But they emerge one by one from the blue fog until hundreds of them gazing at the ship, the ground, the rain falling on their new home.

And I see Father.

No older than five or six in human years. He limps from the blue fog suspiciously. Even as a child, the force of his personality is obvious. And something else, too: the harshness of a boy devastated by war who has taken refuge within a hard emotional shell.

An older woman (my grandmother?) steps up and takes his hand. Father reluctantly accepts her touch, scowl deepening.

An older man is the last to step from the blue haze into the rain. He addresses the group in a weird combination of sound and energy. But, somehow, I understand what he is saying. That Chronox scouts have found places for them within the mainstream of the human time-flow and are awaiting them there. The refugees begin winking out, vanishing one at a time until only the old man remains. Satisfied his charges are safely on their way, he steps up to the silver egg-ship and presses a button on its side before vanishing in a blink of light.

The craft super-heating to a bright orange glow and vaporizing with a muted scream is the last thing I see before Tipping to follow them.

~ * ~

Under the direction of the older man, their leader, Anspach, the Chronox refugees find homes for themselves in eras that suit their temperament, their delight, their capability for survival. Always there is a tacit understanding: they will not use their abilities to Tip to harm or gain unfair advantage over their human hosts. Again and again, Anspach reminds them: they are guests here. Guests.

Father is brought into the mid-Twentieth Century. The choice made by grandmother does not seem to suit him. His suspicions deepen as he is given clothes, a home, a human life to lead. But bubbling beneath, always that wave of anger. And then…

~ * ~

"There's something wrong with him. He feels nothing!"

I flinch away from the sound of someone kicking a wall by flattening myself against the back of the closet in Father's boyhood home.

"Steven, try to understand. Andrew has been through a lot for a boy his age."

"We've all been through a lot! We've all had the Adjustment to deal with, But, Kira, he's sick. We're all struggling to learn to get along with humans, yet your son—"

"Our son, Steven."

"*Your* son goes and does this to his classmate! How are we supposed to keep our presence here a secret if he continues behaving this way?"

He pauses and I hear Elvis Presley singing "Hound Dog" to a group of adoring fans on the TV.

"He's upset."

"Upset, okay. Fine! That I can understand. But, Kira, we arrived at this world like thieves in the night. These beings don't even know we exist! Or about the power we could have over them if we chose! But, you know, I don't think that even matters. They'd welcome us even if they knew we were here. Because they're good."

"Well, I don't know if I'd go that far."

"Plain, simple, superstitious, primitive. Foolish, accidentally destructive. Ridiculously ignorant of the universe and their place in it! But ultimately and fundamentally good. We have—"

"Steven—"

"We have an obligation to obey their laws and avoid hurting them!"

"But the girl was teasing him!"

"Teasing him? So what? That's no excuse for what he did! He's going to have to learn to not use his power against humans."

"And you think punishing him is the way?"

"How else is he going to understand his mistakes? Call him in."

As grandmother calls Father, I draw a deep breath and push the closet door open a crack. I watch Father cross the hall from the kitchen with his head down but that angry look I remember from his arrival on Earth still smoldering in his eyes. He has aged a few years and filled out to become a big boned eleven-year-old. He does not glance toward me as he stalks into the living room.

"…understand why what you did was wrong, don't you, Andrew?" I hear the question resolve out of the indistinct buzz of conversation.

"Yeah! Yeah, I get it."

"Okay. Then perhaps you could explain it to me."

Father says nothing.

"Andrew, humans exist in time. It is all they have. To rob them of it—"

"To hell with humans! To hell with this planet and everything on it! Let it burn. To hell with you!"

The rage in those words. They flow out the door to touch me where I crouch against the wall, eavesdropping. Father will never listen to reason. He is immune to compassion. Father simply hates his new home and the beings inhabiting it with a fury that is elemental.

"All right, Andrew. You leave me with no alternative."

Light blazes in jagged edges on the lintel and threshold. I creep down the hall to the living room doorway. A blaze of Discontinuity hangs in the air. Within its flaming aperture, an image of Father, much younger, frowning suspiciously as his mother takes his hand by the silver spaceship on the grassy plain in India 8,000 years before.

"You're going back, Andrew. I'm sorry, but I'm going to Tip you back to the age of six again to relive the last five years. It's the most difficult punishment any Chronox can inflict on their child. It is going to hurt us more than it's going to hurt you. But you must go back and learn the lessons you failed to learn in your first five years here. You must learn how to get along with humans. You must learn not to be cruel to them."

I watch as he begins pushing Father toward the blazing golden hole in time. In the instant before touching the Discontinuity and melting into his former self, Father twists against Steven's leg until he is facing the door where I watch.

Our eyes meet. And I see in his, a hate vaster than all the oceans of the world.

~ * ~

Steven's punishment does not work. For five years, Father relives ages six to eleven, brooding on his mistakes. He waits. Instead of making Father less cruel, Steven's punishment only teaches him to be more cautious.

~ * ~

Father meets Uncle Leo in college.

Where Father is dark and slender and tends toward ominous silences, Leo is brawny and animated and given to declaring his presence in loud tones. Both hate humans.

"What's the goddamned point of being Chronox if we can't turn it to our advantage?" Leo hisses one winter afternoon in the campus library.

Most of the students have gone home for the holidays. The grounds of the university are deserted. The two young men are alone in maintaining a hum of intellectual activity and purpose among the ivory towers.

"My step-father's so old-guard about the whole thing," Father complains. "'Oh, the humans have been so nice to us so we mustn't harm them…'"

"Don't you hate that shit?"

"'They live in space and time!'"

"Primitive."

"I mean—come on! They're fucking animals. I don't live on the same level as a cow or cat. Why should I accept life among humans as my lot? We could own this world if we tried!"

"Wouldn't take much."

Hidden between two stacks of books close by the study table at which the two converse, below posters of rock concerts, and Vietnam anti-war leaflets, voices low although the library is empty, I witness the germ of all that is to come.

"The problem," Father says, "would be guys like Steven, my step-dad, and the majority of 'moral', 'well-intentioned' human-loving Chronox here and at CenterPoint. Under Anspach's leadership, they'd stand against us. They'd say—"

"'It was their world first so we should allow them to run it!'" Leo laughs. "The problem would be that they'd use their own power to Tip to frustrate us. We can't go back and change history. And we can't go forward into the future because Anspach has decreed that's 'bad'. So we'd have to…?"

"We'd have to come up with a way to prevent their traveling to certain points in time. Or else come up with an alternate way of Tipping that only we can control. Like—say we put timegates around certain key moments in time? Nobody could come in or out except us; using our specialized method."

"How about technology? A time machine? Surely, we could figure out how to build one."

"We'd need a test subject. Preferably a Chronox. But where to find one? That's the question. Plus, it would take a lot of money."

Leo laughs. "Figure out a way to make the humans pay for it!"

They both find that hilarious. Father's laughter rises to echo from the stone walls of the empty library.

I begin edging away. I am so engrossed in being quiet I fail to notice the book cart until I jar it with a loud bang.

"What was that?" Leo snaps.

Father surges to his feet and begins searching. On tiptoe, I sidle around the elevator bank to the stairwell and slip inside, remaining flat against the wall beside the window until he passes. Then, satisfied I am safe, I step toward the stairs.

Movement outside. I look.

A squad of Phoenix/Gold soldiers sprints toward the library through the rain. I turn to find a quiet spot in which to Tip when a distant figure catches my eye.

There, by the entrance to the Student Union, a large man in ice-cream-colored pants and shirt, a thin tie dangling from around his neck, is selling balloons from an outlandishly red cart. From a distance of perhaps a quarter mile, I see him turn in my direction. Smile. And wave.

~ * ~

I can run. But I can't hide much longer. They're closing in on me, now. I need to take precautions. Getting a gun is no problem. When you can Tip through Time and Space at will, obtaining an unregistered firearm is a breeze.

I ride the Discontinuity to the aftermath of a battle in mid-Twentieth Century Russia and pick my way through the debris and of a dead Waffen-SS soldier. I lift his Walther pistol. Taking a gun from a dead Nazi fills me with a flush of poetic justice. (Hitler, after all, apparently wasn't such a bad guy.) And I Tip.

~ * ~

The gun weighs down the pocket of my windbreaker as I stand on the beach in Acapulco ten years after Father's conversation with Uncle Leo in the library. The night wind sweeps the deserted sands. Disco music filters down from the lit hotel patio where, scant hours before, Father exchanged marriage vows with Mother in a ceremony before a small circle of friends.

Now that he is alerted to my flight through time, I know he'll be looking for me. One way to survive a shark is to be like the pilot fish: swim too close to the hunter's side to be recognized as prey. I knew Father would never think to look for me here. I have a destination toward which I am edging in slow stages.

Meanwhile, it is a lovely evening. Acapulco rings the crescent beach in a necklace of light. Waves hush and withdraw. The crescent moon hangs. Her voice is directly behind me:

"Chris."

I turn.

Fist on hip and shoes in hand, Tara stands about three meters away, radiating impatience.

"Trouble-maker. Little...*asshole!*"

As always, I say nothing.

"You know we've got close to a dozen teams combing the time streams for you? Do you realize how much time you're taking up? Wasteful, spoiled, disgusting little—"

"Good, Tara! I'm glad I'm taking up all your precious time! Because God knows, you've stolen enough of mine!"

I scream with pent-up fury and a lifetime of humiliation unleashed.

Her mouth softens into a dangerous smile. "What did you think? Hmm, Chris? Do you honestly imagine that's even possible to stop what's been put in motion?"

"Maybe!"

"Ha! Billions of dollars have been sunk into this Project. The combined weight of the Western democracies and NATO are behind it! Every day, more and more Chronox surrender to our cause or are neutralized. And what? You imagine a pathetic little boy can stand against all that? It's ridiculous.

"Chris, entire nations have been taken down in support of this Project. And you'll be no different. Once we go back, you'll undergo an operation that'll make it impossible for you to Tip ever again.

Then you'll be tucked away somewhere permanently. Time out for you. For good."

"You'll have to catch me first."

"I already have. I've been Tipping a lot longer than you. There's no way you can out-Tip or out-run me now! And if we fight? Guess who's earned her black belt from Airman Ryerson? That's right!"

Tara smiles and executes a mocking karate bow.

"So you see, Chris, I've beaten you. Again. Same way I've beaten you in every encounter from the time we were kids! I grew up. You never did! Stupid, stupid, stupid Chris."

She takes a step forward.

"Now come on. Let's—"

In one smooth motion, I draw the Walther and aim at Tara's chest.

Her smile falters.

"Who's stupid now?" I ask coolly. And fire.

~ * ~

It is dark and quiet in the hospital waiting room at two in the morning. A solid inch of snow on the window ledge gleams in the light from the parking lot. A janitor in a blue smock mops the tiles near the stairwell as a lone figure sits reading a newspaper in the chair by the nurses' station.

Father.

At first, I considered wearing some sort of disguise for our big show-down. But then I realized it wouldn't be much of a show-down if he didn't know who I was. The man I am meeting is five scant years into marriage; a male Chronox in his late twenties encumbered with a new mortgage, struggling with the politics of his first real post-college job and waiting for his wife to give birth to a baby.

Me.

I have arrived at my destination.

I approach quietly and take a seat nearby.

"Hi," I say.

He looks up. "Hello," he replies with an air of boredom.

I release the breath I've been holding in a quiet gust.

He has no idea who I am.

"It's awful late for you to be out all by yourself." He glances at his watch. "What brings you here?

"It's my brother. He has cancer."

"Tough luck for him."

"You?"

"My wife's giving birth."

"Congratulations."

"Yeah. Whatever."

"Girl or boy?"

"Mm? A boy. I guess that's a good thing. He'll be of some use to us."

That stings.

"How so?" I ask innocently.

"Well, what about you? Aren't you of help to your family? I mean, with a sick brother and all. You must have to do extra chores and such."

"I help out where I can. But I don't think my parents notice much."

"Why should they? It's their house. You just live in it."

"Well, I think I do a little bit more than just live there. But anyway—what about love?"

"What about it?"

"Well…it's…important. Don't you think? For a parent to love a child? To care—"

"Why?"

I blink.

"Why should a parent care? A child is the result of biological forces, nothing more. It just happens. If you have a child, then use it to your advantage. It has more energy and will outlast you. So use it! Life's too short. You have a responsibility to be good to yourself first."

My jaw muscle tightens. I am overwhelmed with disgust.

"My parents don't feel that way. About my brother, I mean."

He cocks his head, actually listening for what might be the first time in my life.

"They love and care about…Andrew. He was born weak and unhealthy and before his time. He's been in and out of the doctor's office every day of his life. My parents fight to keep him alive with their caring, their love. Every day he makes it through is a triumph. For them. For our family. And when the time comes for me to grow up and have kids, that's how I intend to live. Not like you."

I stand and turn to leave.

I won't kill Father.

He's not worth the bullet.

"Hey," he says as I reach the door.

I turn.

"Andrew's my name."

"What's your son's?"

"I don't know. What's yours?"

"Chris."

"That'll do. Okay, then. Chris. His name is Chris."

I step outdoors into the cold. And from the parking lot, turn and look back through the glass door to where he sits reading the newspaper. Father is then as he has always been: fully, and finally, a stranger to me.

~ * ~

I imagined I'd end it all with a bullet. A dramatic, final gesture that would terminate Father's life and liberate us all from the plans he has for this world. But it turns out you can't solve problems that way and still remain human. Being my Father's son taught me that. So instead I've come here. To the cottage.

It's autumn, now. A quiet period between visits. The lake is still below a darkening sky. A loon cries somewhere in the distance. The boats and furniture have been put away for the season, and a dish rag hangs disconsolately on the wash line. Father's car pulled out of here a few minutes ago. He will not return for several weeks. He just finished installing a new lock on the door behind which sits a prototype of the Tipping Machine.

I know they'll track me here eventually. And when they do, they'll find me with this gas can, sitting beside the charred remains of this building I intend to fill with gasoline and burn to the ground. I will place a timegate around the event, as Kaya taught me, to prevent Father from coming and undoing my sabotage. It won't prevent the artificial aperture of the Jump Slide from opening long enough for the Phoenix/Gold team to rush in and grab me. I'll be dragged back, operated on, and placed in a permanent time out (perhaps even the one I intend to request). And no doubt, Father's former self will find a way to rebuild and begin again. But I will have stopped him. At least for a while.

They buried Lu next door, beside the dock where we first met a small eternity ago. I'm going to finish this now and stow this laptop computer in a waterproof bag next to her grave.

It's 1983. Considering the technology to build one of these machines won't exist for another fifteen years, discovery of the computer should generate some attention. Hopefully that attention will carry over to this document. Someone, somewhere will read it and perhaps even believe it. And begin, however slowly, to figure out how to stop my Father.

It's possible.

Anything is.

Even love.

EPILOGUE
"We are stardust ..."

The foregoing manuscript was discovered on the portable computer excavated from the quarantined site Sierra-3. Analysis and independent verification of the dates and events therein, along with excavation of the ruins and machinery at Sierra-2, continue. Analysts have yet to attribute authorship to the following: a second file from the same computer.

~ * ~

A light rain was falling as Theodore placed the cardboard box on the floor of the VW microbus. Veins of cloud struggled across the pre-dawn sky. No sign of cops or, even better, Mrs. Fazio, their gorgon landlady who's totally uncool insistence upon rent was cramping his tribe's style. So they were fleeing to a commune some friends of Laura's were starting in Vermont. Theodore was tired of the west coast and ready for a change. Besides, there were rumors of a music festival scheduled for August outside of Bethel, New York. He and his ladies planned to make the scene.

"Woodstock" they were calling it.

Theodore couldn't wait.

He took the stairs two at a time to the lobby and ducked inside. *Same old hallway stinking of cheap wine and piss*, he thought. When they'd moved in a year ago, all the units on their floor had been occupied by flower children. But one by one the hippies had drifted away to be replaced by junkies as well as locked doors and fear. No place to raise a kid.

The living room was empty. From the bedroom at the end of the hall, the soft voices of Laura and Sunshine whispered together. Theodore shouldered a box in the kitchen. When he got back to the street, he was surprised to see someone sitting on the front steps.

"Hi, Theodore."

"Chris. Hey!" Theodore stowed the box in the van. "We thought you split for good, man." There was something subtly different about Chris. A wary squint of the eyes. A slight bitterness twisting the lips. He'd been through something bad. Theodore could tell.

"Moving out?" Chris asked.

"Vermont," Theodore replied. It seemed explanation enough. Chris nodded. "Theodore?"

"Yeah?"

"What's today's date?"

"It's…ah…June. Twenty-ninth, I believe. Yeah, man. Rent's due day after tomorrow, so it's the twenty-ninth. That's why we're moving."

"And the year?"

Theodore smiled. "It's 1969, man."

Chris began to cry. Quietly, at first, and without movement: just a trickle of tears coursing down his cheeks to his chin. But soon he was sobbing with volcanic force, each gasp shuddering his body with a storm of grief. Theodore placed a hand on Chris's shoulder and waited. By the time Laura and Sunshine appeared with the last box, the boy was bawling uncontrollably.

No one said a word.

They stowed the last boxes in the van. Theodore took his place behind the wheel. Laura knelt beside Chris and put her arm around his shoulder then gently guided him from the step to a place beside Sunshine, who sat holding the cat in the back seat. Laura smiled at the two children then pushed the panel door shut and took a seat beside Theodore.

The engine started.

Without a backward glance, they drove off down the street and hung a left, headed for Vermont and the rest of that summer.

About the Author

Jamie Mason is the author of several science fiction novels and thrillers. Born in Montreal, he attended the University of Arizona and Chapman University. After a decade spent teaching in the southwest, he returned to Canada in 2005. He has worked variously as a think-tank analyst, a business manager, a professional musician, and a private investigator. Now semi-retired and living in the woods of Vancouver Island, he devotes his time to writing and savoring the vanishing Canadian wilderness.

Learn more @jamiescribbles

More Science Fiction to explore from WolfSinger Publications

Schrodinger's Cat – Eileen Schuh

Chordelia, straddling two of the realities proposed in Everett's Many Worlds Theory of Quantum Physics, has no idea how distorted the line is between choice and fate.

In one of her worlds, Chorie's young daughter is dying—a drama that quickly contaminates her other, much rosier, reality. Before long, the emotional burden of dealing with two separate lives spawns heated legal battles, endangers her role as mother and wife, and causes people in both universes to judge her insane. As her lives begin to crumble, so does Chorie's heart and mind.

When Dr. Penny, a man with disturbing, murky, hypnotic eyes offers to rid her of the life that's causing so much pain, she must decide if she is willing to sacrifice the chance to be with her dying child for the chance to save her marriage and experience happiness.

She thinks she's planned it well—she's researched her choices, prepared herself for the consequences, put everything in place. She makes her decision. However....

Life, as it has the propensity to do, strikes back with the dark and unexpected.

Dispassionate Lies – Eileen Schuh

The year is 2035 and the world's emerging from a devastating economic collapse. Computer guru, Ladesque, finds her task of restoring the world's internet capabilities, dull until…

She's approached by Paul, an attractive FBI agent intent on recruiting her to an ultra-secret project. There's only one problem—the asexuality she was born with thirty-five years ago, vanishes and she's left struggling with the unfamiliar power of libido.

When everyone, from ungainly computer geek, Roach to handsome Paul, becomes appealing, Ladesque suspects the popular explanation for the female asexuality saddling her generation is a lie. Her suspicions increase when an encoded diary and whispered rumours link the affliction to conspiracy and murder. However, uncovering facts proves difficult in an age where hackers have corrupted all digital records.

Putting her quest on hold, she joins Paul's project where her uncertainties are quickly overshadowed by the explosive technology and high-tech challenges of her job. Then, she receives her final assignment. She can either expose her mind to the potentially lethal quantum computer for the sake of the world or be forever a watched woman.

She, alone, must assess the risk—a risk that just might reveal the truth about her past.

The Station – A. David Smith

The distant future. Humanity has reached the stars…and found no life. On a remote space station, lone crewman Lt. Robert Bradley awakens to starless space and complete darkness.

When he summons the courage to venture outside, Bradley becomes the first human to embark on humanity's greatest journey. He will develop a new understanding of the universe and witness the destinies of countless sentient life forms.

Bonded Agent – David B. Riley

They say graduates of the Martian School of Economics really go places. That's certainly true for Sarah Meadows. After taking a job with the Gompers Insurance Company they send her to weapons training on her second day on the job. She's soon parachuting out of spaceships, hunting down cargo pirates and even trying to salvage a derelict vessel that may be haunted. Not to mention getting involved in a war between Earth and a reptilian race.

Indigo – Joy Jones

A world decimated by virus. A crime lord's daughter holds

the key. Can she discover it in time?

Meet the crime lord of the future—she's five foot five, wears an evening gown, has computerized reflexes, and carries a Glock. Her soldados defend her against assassination or attacks by San Francisco homeless. But neither they nor the world of high tech Jaymes lives in can protect her from GEORG—a virus that thinks and plans, or Adan Bernardo, the mysterious scientist behind it.

When her corporate stronghold comes crashing down, she's forced to make new and bizarre friends with talents for manipulating technology to uncover her family skeletons and how they link to a terrible future. Unless, that is, Jaymes can unlock the secret she carries within herself to fight back.

Her world depends on it.

Project W.Olf – Eileen Schuh

Wildlife biologist, Peter Kane, would much rather be in the wilderness studying his wolves but he's committed to his role as a research subject for the Wainwright University's Olfactory Project.

The extension of the project has left him short of cash so although things haven't worked out between him and Marie, when the police need his nose for their investigation into her past, he reluctantly agrees.

His acute sense of smell proves invaluable and the investigation leaps forward. He's hailed as a hero but when Marie suggests he's a mere pawn in a dangerous conspiracy, he listens. She does, after all, have analytical skills comparable to a supercomputer.

Absolutely nothing, though, can prepare them for the stark truth.

Check them out at www.wolfsingerpubs.com